The Phantom Janitor

by Vincenzo Pasquarella

ISBN 978-1-945247-23-1

THE PHANTOM JANITOR

Copyright © 2017 by Vincenzo Pasquarella

First Edition, 2017. All rights reserved.

A Thurston Howl Publications Book
Published by Thurston Howl Publications
thurstonhowlpublications.com
Lansing, MI

jonathan.thurstonhowlpub@gmail.com

Edited by Kaelan
Cover artist: Rov

Printed in the United States of America
10 9 8 7 6 5 4 3 2 1

Before you start reading, I want to use this page to dedicate this book to all of the people who inspired me and helped me as I went through the process of bringing this idea to print. Whether it was through just support, love, and encouragement; advice; beta reading; or picking up the book and reading it, I want to thank you so much. I hope you enjoy this book.

Chapter 1

Electric guitar music blared from Derrick Hilman's cell phone to the tune of "Phantom of the Opera." He lifted his head from his pillow with a tired smile on his face and rested it on his arm, just listening to the music with his eyes closed and his head nodding.

A pillow came flying from the other side of the room and hit Derrick in the face. "Come on dude! Turn that off. Let me just get a few more minutes of sleep." His roommate Frankie put his pillow over his ears and flopped back down on his bed. Frankie was a snow leopard and Derrick's best friend and roommate. An uncontrollable flirt, Frankie couldn't get a girl to like him no matter how hard he tried. He also had a reputation for opening his mouth and inserting his foot, especially when he talked to other species or females.

Frankie was also Derrick's roommate because he couldn't live at his stepdad's house anymore . . . due to family issues. He growled a little and tossed in his bed, "Derrick, I love you man, but you need to stop listening to show tunes."

Derrick rolled his eyes and scratched his head. "Why?"

"Listen, I am grateful you came to live with me after all the bad stuff that happened to you, but you are a geek."

Derrick reluctantly turned off the alarm. "Oh, come on, you're no fun. I love show tunes, especially that song."

Frankie mumbled, "Hey, are you going to the hospital to see your mom today?"

Derrick shook his head. "Ernesto said the staff won't let me in unless she asks for me." His alarm went off again, and he chuckled as he quickly turned it off again.

Frankie sat back up; his fur was a mess on his head, and his eyes narrowed. "How can you listen to that? You've lived here for two years, and you've woken up to that noise every single morning." He rubbed his eyes and whined. "I wanna go back to sleep."

Derrick sprang from his bed and yawned. He stretched and feigned checking his phone, a fun plan to get his friend up and out of bed forming in his mind. "Well, okay. But you're gonna miss the first day of the new school year. Rowley's already there."

Their young kangaroo friend, Rowley, had a strong Australian accent and a love for books and vegetables. Rowley had been Derrick's more headstrong friend since they met, and Rowley usually helped keep Derrick out of dangerous situations. Especially ones with his step-dad.

Derrick smirked, "He said something about a foreign exchange student from France." Derrick turned and stretched his back so his friend wouldn't see his smirk. "And she's a dingo."

Frankie fell out of bed and looked up with a really wide grin. "New girl? Dingo?" He sprang up and rushed around the room, getting ready for school.

Derrick chuckled and grabbed his clothes and went into the bathroom to take a shower. "That guy is so gullible."

Derrick walked into the kitchen, having showered and put on clean clothes, ready to face the day.

Frankie stood on a chair, rummaging through the cupboard. He turned and glared. "Dude, did you eat my pop-tarts again? They aren't where I put them!"

Derrick shook his head, "Nope. I didn't eat your pop-tarts. Did you check the fridge? That's where I suggested you put them."

Frankie glanced at him suspiciously, then got off the chair and opened the fridge. He frowned at the open box of pop-tarts inside. "You DID eat one! I knew it. The box was closed when I bought it, and I haven't eaten any yet."

Derrick chuckled, "Maybe I did eat one."

Frankie grabbed one of the packages from the box in the fridge, ripped it open, and growled, baring his teeth. "Mine!" He pointed at Derrick, "You. No. Touch. My. Pop-tarts."

Derrick rolled his eyes, "Frankie, don't talk like that. I. Can't. Understand. If. You. Cut. Off. At. Every. Word."

Frankie cocked his head at his friend as he ate his pop-tart. "Dude, can you not talk like that? I can't understand you if you cut off your sentence at every word." He took another bite of his pop-tart.

Derrick rolled his eyes again and whacked the snow leopard on the back of the head. "Oh, can't you?" He chuckled. "Come on, we're gonna be late for school. Rowley's gonna jump off the walls if that happens. Probably quite literally." He walked out the door, then realized something and peeked back in, "Frankie."

Frankie looked up. "Yeah?"

"You left the fridge open. Can you close it?"

Frankie looked at the door, "Oh! Um . . ." He closed the fridge door with a dreamy smile on his face.

"Come on. Let's go." Derrick smiled and patted the leopard on the back.

"We're going to go see the dingo girl, right?"

Derrick laughed, "Oh, I forgot to mention . . . I lied about that." He walked out the front door.

Frankie looked up at the ceiling and yelled, "Why do I always fall for that?" He walked out the door, grumbling under his breath.

Frankie drove his truck into the school parking lot.

Derrick looked up at Tigerthorn High. For some reason, it looked bigger than he had remembered it, but then again . . . a new year could do that to a dog.

"You wanna hear something funny? Last year, I couldn't wait to get out of this place, and now I can't wait to get back." Frankie put his paw on the window as he stared out at the school.

Derrick chuckled "You only have three courses this year, and none of them are math!" He nudged him. "Maybe that has something to do with it?"

But Frankie wasn't listening to him; he was too busy looking out at all the people walking around the campus, mainly the girls. "Dude, there are so many new girls. Senior year is gonna be so much fun!"

Derrick shook his head at his friend, got out of the truck, and slammed the door, breaking his friend out of his trance. "Come on, Romeo. We've got to find Rowley."

Frankie glared. "Dude! Don't slam the door like that."

Derrick searched the school for their Australian friend, but he didn't see the kangaroo anywhere. "I don't see him, do you?" He didn't get an answer, so he turned to look at Frankie and saw him talking to a cheetah. He facepalmed. "Typical. We go to look for Rowley, he goes to add another phone number to his contacts." He walked over to them.

The cheetah looked very uncomfortable, but she smiled gratefully when Derrick dragged Frankie back to looking for Rowley. "Frankie. We have to find Rowley before class starts. He has our schedules, and if we don't get them now, we're going to be wandering around all day looking for our classes." He turned to look around the courtyard. "Now help me look for . . ."

Suddenly, a yell interrupted Derrick's train of thought.

The distant shout grew louder as the noise maker came closer. "GUUUUUUUUUUUUUUUYSSSS!"

He turned to see Rowley hopping toward them with a mischievous grin on his face. Sensing the inevitable collision, Derrick moved out of the way, but Frankie didn't see Rowley and got tackled to the ground by the kangaroo.

Frankie groaned as he laid sprawled on the ground, "Where'd that come from?"

Rowley just sat on Frankie's back, laughing his head off. "G'day mates!"

Derrick smiled and offered the Aussie his paw to help him up.

Rowley took it and got off Frankie's back. "Sorry, Frankie! Just a l'il jumpy." He took a school football out of his backpack. "Guess who's a Tigerthorn Tiger?"

Frankie bounced up from the ground, "You made the team?" He asked excitedly.

Rowley grinned and nodded, "Cain held tryouts at 5:30 this morning. You're looking at the new center and kicker for the Tigerthorn Tigers!"

Derrick clapped him on the back. "That's awesome, Rowley! I knew you could do it!"

Rowley smiled a huge smile and hugged them both, "I still can't believe . . ."

"Hey twerp trio!" yelled an all too familiar voice.

Derrick, Frankie, and Rowley turned to see Razor and his two cronies, Manny and Buck. Razor was a white tiger, Manny was a hyena, and Buck was . . . a buck. They had two joined interests; they loved playing football, and they loved teasing Derrick and Frankie. They used to make fun of Rowley, too, but then he joined them in playing football, and they ended up warming up to him. But they still made fun of him for his company.

Razor walked up to them with a sneer on his face. "You're back for another year? You're either really brave or really stupid."

Derrick looked him in the eye, "Well, I am not as dumb as you are, so we all know which one I am."

Razor's eyes narrowed, "What did you just say?" He grabbed Derrick's shirt by the collar and raised his fist to punch him in the nose.

Manny put a paw on Razor's shoulder and pointed to the other side of the courtyard. "R-raze . . . Cain's watching . . ."

Razor and Derrick turned to look toward the other end of the courtyard and saw the dark shadow of a large wolf glaring at them. Razor's eyes widened. He glared back at Derrick, "This isn't over, timber wolf." He walked off toward the school. Manny and Buck trembled as they followed after their friend to their class.

Derrick looked across the courtyard and smiled at the figure. The wolf nodded, and he moved away into the school. Derrick shivered, "That guy is creepy. The way he can disappear like that."

Frankie shrugged, "Yeah, let's not talk about that right now. The guy kind of haunts my nightmares already."

Derrick jolted as he saw Cain appear again, as if it had somehow heard Frankie, and glared at them. "Dude . . . I think he heard you, Frankie . . . Have no idea how, but he's there again."

Frankie shivered, "The guy is like Batman . . ." He gave the shadow one last glance and turned toward the building, "Come on . . . we're going to be late."

Derrick nodded, and they walked into the school.

As they walked through the hallways of the school, Derrick could hear everyone's conversations as they passed by.

"It's all over the news." One of the cheerleaders squealed.

"She's coming back to finish her senior year! Here. At Tigerthorn."

". . .Setting up a big acting competition." his step-sister Lorena said to her friends.

His ears perked up at that last part, and he walked up to her. "What? What's going on?"

Lorena gave him a look. "Did I invite you into this conversation, 'Dirt for Brains'?"

Lorena Claw . . . The apple of her dad's eye. Derrick had use many words he used to describe her in his head, and most of them were not nice. Regardless, he felt they best reflected her . . . colorful personality. She shared her dad's hatred for the timber wolf and tried as hard as she could to be as rude to Derrick as possible so her dad could be proud of her.

He crossed his arm impatiently. "Did the Titanic invite the iceberg along for its maiden voyage and then let it crash into it and sink, killing hundreds of people? No, but it did anyway. So, I'm going to ask again, what is going on?"

Lorena and her friends laughed, "You think you're so tough now, don't you. Wait till my dad hears about your smart mouth. He'll work you and your loser friends till midnight for weeks!"

Derrick turned and walked away.

"But if it'll shut you up . . ."

Derrick turned back toward her with an eyebrow raised, waiting for her to go on.

"Cassidy Wells is coming back to do her senior year here, and she's holding a big acting competition." She gave him the once-over and smirked. "But why someone like you would need to know something like that, I don't even know . . . or care."

Derrick's heart stopped when he heard her name. "S-she's coming back to school? Here?!" He stammered. His mind raced. Cassidy? Coming back to town? His tail started wagging as his mind drifted to the girl he had been crushing on since he stopped thinking girls were weird. He could remember the day that he first met her . . . and the day he let her go.

Cassidy Wells, the Alaskan Husky. Derrick had been head over heels for her since the day he met her. She had been the prettiest girl in his class when they went to school together five years before. She loved acting, reading books to elementary students, hanging out with Derrick when no else would, and actually thought he was an amazing actor.

Sadly, that was how they ended up parting ways. Cassidy had been anxious to try out for an acting competition and had wanted Derrick to be her acting partner, but he . . . being extremely insecure, ran out on her. So, she ended up joining the competition with a friend, and they actually won. In doing so, they caught the eye of an agent. He offered her and her friend a contract, and they were off to Hollywood. Derrick ended up not seeing Cassidy again except in movies. Until today.

Lorena's smirk got bigger as she watched him, "Aww! Someone has a crush." She put a paw on his shoulder, "I'm going to just tell you this now." She whispered in his ear, "She's never, EVER going to like someone like you."

Derrick's head and tail drooped.

One of Lorena's friends noticed and laughed, "Awwwww, look! The poor puppy is sad."

Lorena chuckled and glared at Derrick, "Poor thing!" She shoved him against the lockers, "Maybe someone should just put it down." She turned to her friends, "Come on. We're done here." They followed her to their class.

Derrick just stood against the lockers. His heart burned with a stabbing pain as if his step-sister had shoved a knife right into it. He knew she didn't really know . . . but being told the girl you like will never like you still hurts like hell.

Rowley came and stood beside him and gave him a hug. "It's okay, mate; you'll be okay. You can't let some ugly ol' jackal take you down."

Frankie walked to the other side of Derrick and clapped him on the back, "Yeah! She's probably wrong about Cassidy, anyway. She doesn't know Cassidy. She probably can't wait to see you again."

Derrick smiled at his friends and hugged them both, "You guys are the best friends I could ever ask for."

Rowley smiled, "And don't'cha forget it, mate!" He chuckled, "Come on. We've got 12th grade English for our first class. Room A-21."

Derrick sat in his assigned seat, tapping his pencil on his desk and waiting for the class to start.

Rowley, who sat in the desk next to him, whispered at him. "PSST! Hey mate! Can I borrow one of your pencils? Someone just told me that Mrs.

Hatfield is a stickler about forgetting writing utensils."

Derrick nodded and got him a pencil from his bag. "Just don't break it."

Rowley chuckled and took the pencil and feigned smashing it against the table.

Derrick smiled and rolled his eyes.

The door near the front of the classroom opened, and the teacher walked in. A tall jaguar, Mrs. Hatfield liked wearing gray skirts, sweaters, and wearing her hair tied up in a bun. Though she looked rough, she always had a knack for having fun in her classes.

She stood before the class and smiled cheerfully at the class. "Good morning class! My name is Mrs. Hatfield. Since this is your last year of high school, we are going to be learning 12th Grade English. This year, I am hoping to help strengthen and sharpen your reading and writing skills by teaching you intensively about the rules of grammar. But of course, I'm going to throw a little bit of fun into it so it isn't boring." She took out her roll sheet. "Now, I'm going to call roll; when I say your name, just let me know you're here by a little wave."

Derrick sat in his chair as she called roll. When she said his name, he raised his paw. She got through the roll and then went on to say something that made Derrick's heart stop.

"And I'm sure that we're all thrilled to have the lovely Cassidy Wells join us for class this year." Mrs. Hatfield smiled and pointed to the back of the room. Derrick heard the sound of someone clearing their throat. She rolled her eyes, "Oh, and her friend, Elena."

Elena was a Bengal Tiger and probably one of the sassiest and most violent people he knew. Her favorite things to do were singing and beating up people who hurt her friends. She was the friend who loved to tease Derrick about his shyness but could always give good advice when the situation called for it; usually blunt and truthful advice no one wanted to follow. But Derrick didn't actually hear her name. He only heard Cassidy's.

Derrick stayed frozen in his seat. She was there right now, in the back of the room! He had to painfully resist the urge to turn around because his face heated up. It had been five years; she probably wouldn't even remember him. But that didn't change the fact that she sat somewhere back there. He wasn't going to be able to avoid her. He almost froze thinking about her.

Lost in thought about Cassidy, He didn't notice Mrs. Hatfield trying to get his attention. "Derrick? Hello? Earth to Derrick?"

Derrick gave his head a shake and looked up at his teacher, "I'm sorry . . . What?"

The class giggled.

Mrs. Hatfield frowned, "I asked you if you were alright. You don't look so good."

Derrick sighed, not even slightly "alright". He could not seem to get the girl of his dreams out of his head. He looked in the direction of her voice, but all he could see were blurs. "No . . . ma'am."

Rowley gave Derrick a worried look, then turned to the teacher and raised his paw. "Mrs. Hatfield, can Frankie and I take Derrick to the nurse's office?"

Mrs. Hatfield nodded, "Yes, go on."

Frankie and Rowley got up from their desks and helped Derrick out of his seat and to the door.

As they walked down the hallway, Rowley looked at his friend as they helped him along. "You must really like her. You were only in the room with her for five minutes before you heard her name and froze up."

Derrick wasn't listening, though, his head spinning faster than a top.

Frankie waved a paw in front of his friend's face, then looked at Rowley. "Oh man, he's really out of it. I've never seen him like this. He's worse than you get around girls.

Rowley ignored his friend's jab, "Not relevant, Frankie. I don't know . . ."

Before Rowley could finish his thought, a soft, feminine voice cut him off. "Derrick?"

Derrick stopped abruptly. He knew that voice; he had thought he would never hear it ever again. He turned around, and his heart beat increased. It hammered in his chest, and he couldn't remember how to breathe.

Cassidy Wells stood behind them with Elena at her side. "Derrick Hilman? Is that you? Is that really you?"

Derrick gaped at her, "C-C-Cassidy?" He put a paw on his head and tried to walk toward her, swaying one way and then another, stumbling down the hallway towards. But halfway there, the world tilted and rippled, and his vision went black as he passed out.

His friends gathered around him, looking down at him. Elena grinned and elbowed Cassidy. "Yeah, I am pretty sure that's Derrick."

Chapter 2

DERRICK WOKE UP IN THE nurse's office. His head hurt a little, but other than that he was okay. He turned his head to see Rowley sitting in a chair next to the nurse's table Derrick laid on. Derrick sat up abruptly, which only made his head hurt worse.

Rowley sat up when he saw Derrick had woken up, "Glad you're up! You scared us out there, mate. You okay?"

Derrick winced at the throbbing pain in his head, "My head really hurts . . . Ugh! I am so pathetic . . ."

Rowley handed him a tablet of painkiller and a cup of water. "Here. The nurse wanted you to take this when you woke up. And don't you dare tell me that."

Derrick took the painkiller and drained all the water out of the cup and cringed at the awful taste of the medicine. "But I am. I passed out in the middle of the hallway."

Rowley shook his head, "That doesn't mean anything. You passed out, everyone else does it at some point. Listen to me. Pathetic people don't have friends. I'm your friend, Frankie is your friend; so, don't you dare say you're pathetic." His serious expression slowly melted into a smirk, "Or I'll tackle you." He offered Derrick his paw, "Come on, everyone is waitin' for you outside."

Derrick smiled, took Rowley's paw, and slid off the table. "Have I ever told you you're one of my best friends in the entire world?"

Rowley crossed his arms and held his head high. "I reckon that has already been established."

Derrick rubbed his head as the pain slowly went away, "How long have

I been out?"

Rowley shrugged as he opened the door to the office, "No worries, mate. You were only out for ten minutes."

Derrick walked through the door into the main office and saw Frankie, Elena, and . . . "Cassidy!"

She looked up as he walked in and smiled at him. A genuine smile, she actually looked happy to see him. "Derrick!" She rushed from her seat to give him a hug.

His eyes widened, but he didn't resist. Instead, he hugged back with a smile on his face. She was really there, and her arms were around him. Derrick almost pinched himself to make sure he'd actually woken up.

She pulled away and looked at him, "Oh my gosh, you've changed so much. It's been so long. I've missed you."

His heart thumping in his chest. She had missed him! "I-I missed you too, Cass . . . How've you been?"

Cassidy smiled at the use of her old nickname, "I've been doing okay . . . Made some friends in Hollywood, but they were nothing like my friends here, and I missed you guys so much! So, when my agent gave me time off from acting so I could come home to finish High School in a familiar community, I couldn't have gotten back here faster." She pulled Rowley over and hugged them both. "I missed my three buddies."

He chuckled, closing his eyes and hugging her back.

Rowley looked at his shoes and said nothing, looking pretty nervous. He usually got like this around girls.

Cassidy pulled away and smiled, "What about you guys?" She looked at Derrick, "How's your mom doing? Any better?"

Derrick's face fell. "N-no. She's still alive, though. Really happy about that." He chuckled nervously.

Cassidy grinned, "Yeah. That's great." She looked down at the ground as if trying to figure out what to say next.

Elena stood up and walked over to Derrick and punched him in the arm. "Derrick! My bro, so glad to see you ain't passed out anymore."

Derrick winced and rubbed his arm, "Hey, Elena. Still got the punch, I see."

Elena smirked, "Yep. I had a lot of practice." She grinned, "I'm a good stuntwoman." She put her arm around Rowley's neck. "It's good to be back, though. Now, I can beat up on the idiots here." She gave Rowley a flirtatious smile, laughing a little when he started fidgeting. "Hey, Rowley, still as shy as ever?" She kissed him on the cheek, making him squirm a little more.

Cassidy rolled her eyes, "Elena, cut it out! You're making him nervous."

Elena sighed and took her arm off his back. "Fine." she grumbled but gave Rowley a wink as she backed off.

Cassidy looked at the clock. "Oh! We have to get back to class. We've been gone for twenty-five minutes. Mrs. Hatfield's gonna give us detention." She walked toward the office door. "We can catch up more during lunch."

Frankie, who had been sitting nearest to the door, opened it for her.

Cassidy smiled and walked out, followed by Elena.

Frankie waited until they were a ways down the hallway before turning to Rowley, who still looked nervous. "Man . . . You handled that well, Rowley."

Rowley glared at Frankie, "Shut up. C'mon, let's go back to class."

Derrick looked at them both, Frankie's little smirk and Rowley's glare, but he didn't think much about it. He thought about Cassidy and how fun this year would end up being now.

Derrick got up from his seat and stretched.

Rowley sprang to his side in a second. "Come on mate. It's lunchtime. We get to sit with the girls!"

Elena walked up to them and smirked, "Funny, you're never this excited when we're actually around. You're usually shy and quiet." Rowley jumped and backed away, stammering. She smiled at him. "There's our Rowley! The Australian cutie."

Rowley hid behind Derrick and mumbled, "Stop it . . ."

Cassidy came up behind her, "Elena! Come on. Stop messing with my buddy!" She held her arms out for a hug. "Come here, Rowley."

Rowley peeked out and walked over to give Cassidy a hug.

Cassidy smiled, "See? No need to be nervous around girls." She whispered in his ear, but loud enough so Elena and Derrick could hear too. "It lets them know you like them."

Rowley's eyes went wide, and he stood up straight, trying to hide his nerves. "Sorry guys . . . It's just really hot in here . . ."

Elena nodded with a knowing grin, "Mmhmm . . ." She walked outside.

Derrick laughed and put an arm around his friend. "Come on, Rowley. She has the right idea, and I am starving." He offered his paw to Cassidy, "You coming?"

She smiled and took it. "Of course, I am."

Cassidy smiled as she walked down the hallway with Derrick and Rowley. For the first time in five years, she was back with the people that she cared about. She had really missed them: Rowley, his chipper accent and tendency to get nervous around girls; Frankie and his hilarious attempts at flirting; and Derrick.

She and Derrick had a special friendship back before she left; one she hoped to continue now that she had returned. They had parted on such a bad note, and she wanted her friend back. Something about the timber wolf drew her to him. He had a very kind personality, he had what she called mathematical magic, he loved to act (in her opinion, he acted well), and he had such an adorable smile.

As she walked down the hallway holding his paw, she looked at him and caught him staring at her. When he saw she had noticed, he looked away with a chuckle. He had been acting a little weird, with the fainting and stuff. But as Elena had said before, that was Derrick.

They saw Frankie waiting for them near the door to the lunchroom, and as they got closer, Cassidy let her paw slip from Derrick's.

She walked toward Frankie, giving him a small wave, when someone grabbed her paw.

"Welcome back, Cassidy."

Cassidy turned to see Razor behind her. "Oh . . . Razor. Hi."

Razor smiled, "Is that it? You haven't seen me in five years, and all you can say is that?"

Derrick walked over and pulled Razor away, "Dude, can't you see she's uncomfortable?"

Razor turned on him, "No one asked for your input, Mr. Janitor Boy. Now run along, Miss Cassidy and I have some unfinished business." He turned back to Cassidy and started massaging her paw. "Don't we?"

Cassidy tensed as Razor came closer, and his paws were rubbing her arm. His paws on her made her stomach lurch. Apparently, the jock had no concept of personal space. She tried to jerk her paw away. "Stop it, Razor."

Derrick put his paw on Razor's shoulder, "The lady said stop."

Razor turned and punched Derrick in the stomach, "Heel boy."

Derrick groaned and knelt to the ground. "Ouch."

Razor pointed into the lunchroom. "Go. Now."

Cassidy watched as Derrick gave her a hangdog look and limped toward the cafeteria, Rowley helping him along.

Razor turned back with a smile, "I'm sorry about him. Doesn't know when to keep his mouth . . ."

Suddenly, an angry Elena pulled Razor away from Cassidy by the collar of his shirt. "Hello, Razor." She said with a growl, holding Razor by the collar of his shirt.

Razor swallowed, and he tried to smile. "Elena! Oh . . . Hey. How've you been? You miss me?"

Elena smirked, "Oh, I missed you alright." She reeled her free fist back and punched him in the face. She let go of his collar, and he fell to the ground groaning, holding his nose. "I missed doing that to you, that's for sure."

Cassidy smiled and high fived Elena. "Thanks! I'm really glad you're on my side."

Elena chuckled. "Everybody is."

A teacher came out of the lunchroom followed by Buck and Manny. "Excuse me? What in Sam's Hill is going on out here?" The teacher yelled, looking from the small crowd to Cassidy and Elena, then at Razor on the ground. "Someone better have a good explanation for this."

Elena crossed her arms and leered at the teacher. "Now you show up?! This dumb jock was all up in my friend's grill without her consent. And he completely sucker punched my buddy Derrick."

The teacher looked a little startled. "Ummm. Violence is discouraged here on school grounds, Miss Salazar. Just because someone starts it doesn't mean you have to finish it. I am going to have to give you detention."

Elena smirked. "Then I guess I'll see you after school." She nodded at Cassidy. "Come on. We have lunch to eat."

Cassidy smiled at her friend, and they walked into the lunchroom. It was a big room full of tables, with a line of students going into the kitchen area. She scanned the room and found Derrick, Rowley, and Frankie sitting at a table. They already had their food and were eating. She glanced at Derrick's table and saw them laugh as Frankie made a joke. She watched as Derrick smiled when Rowley brought up something and took out his football. Derrick . . .

She jolted when Elena nudged her, "What? I'm listening."

Elena pointed to the table closest to the wall, where Buck and Manny were messing with two of the new freshmen. Manny had one of the boys by his collar, and Buck had a firm grip on the other one to keep him from trying to help his friend. She walked up to them.

Manny laughed. "Come on kid, cough up your money, or I will have my buddy over there hurt your friend."

Buck tightened his grip on the other boy, an otter.

The boy hissed in pain as Buck tightened his grip. "Don't do it, Conner. I'll be okay."

Buck gripped tighter, "Shut up kid."

Conner, a wolf, looked at his friend, then back up at Manny. "No wait. Don't hurt Alex! I'll . . ."

"HEY!" Elena interrupted as she walked toward them. "Put the kids down."

Manny looked at Elena and smirked, "Or what, kitty cat?"

Elena gritted her teeth. "I am pretty sure you saw what I did to Razor outside. Do I even need to explain?" She crossed her arm and just stared at Buck, her eyebrows raised, just waiting for him to try her.

Manny's face went blank, and his ears flattened as if he had no idea what he was supposed to do next.

Conner took this opportunity and ran over to Buck and Alex and kicked Buck in the shin. "Let him go." he growled angrily at the buck.

Buck let go of Alex and grabbed his leg. "Owwie owwie owwie!"

Elena came closer, "Go before I clean your clocks."

Buck and Manny backed away terrified and ran to hide behind Razor, who had just staggered in.

Conner yelled after them, "Yeah, you better run!" He turned to Alex, who rubbed his bruised arm. "You okay, man?"

Alex nodded and winced, "Yeah . . . It's just a bruise. He didn't break it." He turned to Elena and Cassidy. He stuck out his paw, "Hi. I'm Alex, and this is my friend, Conner. Thanks for helping us out."

Elena smiled and shook the kid's paw. "No problem, Alex. No one deserves to be bullied on their first day in high school."

Conner's eyes were wide. "Dude! You could be like a superhero?"

Elena's eyes sparkled, "Never thought about it like that. But I'd probably kill it in spandex." She winked at them.

Alex smiled, "Do you want to eat lunch with us? We were about to get some food when those morons tried to mug us with their big muscles and puny brains."

Elena turned to Cassidy with a look, a classic Elena look. The one where she looked like she was begging but not begging. Her eyes were as sad as she could make them without looking pitiful, and she bared her teeth.

Cassidy pretended to pout and nodded. "Fine." Then she saw Derrick look up and raise his eyebrow at them. She sighed and shrugged, gesturing at the kids. He smiled knowingly and gave her a thumbs up.

Elena smirked at the kids, "You know . . . I think we will eat lunch with you today. I like you kids, you're okay."

Conner smiled, "This is gonna be the best year of school ever." He and Alex high fived and got into the lunch line.

Cassidy smiled at them, but shot one last look at Derrick. He looked a little sad. Oh well, she'd have to make it up to him later.

Derrick sighed as he watched Cassidy and Elena talk with the two younger boys in the lunch line as he ate another scoop of his mashed potatoes.

Rowley watched for a second, too, then looked back at his friend. "Well . . . I guess they ain't sittin' with us, then, 'ey mates? No worries! We can still have loads of fun with just us." He smiled a toothy grin and ate a bite of salad.

Frankie shrugged, "I don't know man . . . I missed them while they were away. I was looking forward to hearing some stories."

Derrick beamed. "Well, I am glad that they are gonna be sitting with those two freshmen. Cass is really good at welcoming people to . . . things." He looked over at her again and let himself become entranced by her smile. It was so beautiful; the way she did it just lit up the whole room.

A loud bang brought him out of his reverie. He looked up and saw that

Cain had just put his lunch box on the table and sat down next to Frankie. "Hi."

Derrick smiled, "What's up, Cain?"

Cain gave a low grunt in response.

Razor, Buck, and Manny passed by the table and stopped by Derrick.

Razor growled at Derrick, "Don't you ever get in my way again, Hilman. You hear me? Next time you do, I'll have Buck ram you with his antlers."

Buck nodded, "Yeah, just try and . . ."

Cain opened his lunchbox and pulled out a big container with a huge slab of meat inside it, opened it up, and started eating it.

Buck stopped short when he saw the meat. "W-w-what kind of meat is that?"

Cain looked up at him and tilted his head, biting into a piece. Red juice dribbled from his chin as he bared his teeth at Buck.

Buck's eyes widened, and he fainted.

Razor and Manny gave Cain death glares as they held their friend.

Cain gave them one back, and they yelped and carried their friend back to their table.

Derrick watched them go, then turned back to Cain, "That meat's not as rare as it looks, is it?"

Cain chuckled, "Nope. It's actually Medium Well Done. I marinated it in a mixture of different sauces." He cut another piece and ate it. "You guys want some?" He asked, holding out the container. "I got enough."

Rowley shook his head, "None for me, thank you. I'd rather eat my salad."

Frankie shook his head at Rowley and gave his plate to Cain for a piece of steak. "Herbivores."

Rowley put his paws on his hips. "No offense to the carnivores at this table, but it's better than eating dead things!"

Derrick whispered to Cain, "Are vegetables dead things already?" Cain chuckled a little but said nothing else.

Frankie smirked at Rowley. "Would you rather I eat you?"

Rowley pointed his fork at Frankie, "Try it mate, and you'll get a kick in the face."

Cain nodded, "He's pretty good at that. He kicked a 39-yard field goal during try-outs. He's probably better than most of those other morons that tried out. But I need a team of more than one to win a football game, now, don't I?" He gave Rowley a small smile.

Derrick patted the kangaroo on the back. "That has redeemed you for the carnivore comment."

Rowley put his paws up to defend himself, "Come on, Derrick! I didn't mean ya any harm by that. Only Frankie."

"Ouch."

Frankie rolled his eyes, "You guys are terrible."

Rowley chuckled, "And that's why you hang out with us. We love ya, mate! You're our friend, our extremely gullible, weird friend."

Frankie chuckled in spite of the making fun of him. "Oh! So, I am the weird friend now?" He asked with a smile.

Cain put an arm on his shoulder, "Kid, you've always been the weird friend." He gave him a sharp look, "And I don't need to be like Batman to know that."

Frankie turned white as Rowley and Derrick gaped at him.

Cain ignored their looks for a few seconds, then smiled. "Okay . . . I only overheard you guys because Rowley pocket dialed me."

Rowley face palmed, "OH! I must have done that after jump tacklin' Frankie! Though the fact you didn't just hang up is slightly creepy, too . . ." He chuckled at Frankie's annoyed expression, "Hey! I said I'm sorry."

Cain nodded with a smile, ignoring the second comment. "Yeah, I saw that too. Maybe I should put you on defense as well . . ." He considered it for a few seconds, then laughed and shook his head. "Nah . . . I think I'll let Razor, Buck, and Manny take care of getting the bruises." He glowered at them. "They definitely deserve it."

Derrick nodded in agreement, and he couldn't have agreed more. He knew he shouldn't be like that . . . but they were jerks. Jerks usually got what they gave others. He looked down at his plate. If only Ernesto played defense on the football team with Cain as his coach, then he wouldn't have to be Derrick's boss.

School had let out for the day, and now the three friends were getting yelled at by Ernesto who had stopped by the theater to give the guys a pep talk like every other week. He stood there with a stupid, smug grin. "You guys are going to be unsuccessful idiots, so be grateful you have this job. And seeing as how you each have no talents whatsoever, this is the only place that would take you. Now, you bums need to get to work. Nathan has a whole list of jobs for you." He clapped his paws twice. "Let's go." He walked out of the theater and to his fancy new car.

Derrick bared his teeth at Ernesto. Ernesto Claw, one of the worst beings you could ever meet. The only person Derrick thought was definitely worse than Ernesto was his daughter, Lorena. But Ernesto was still pretty bad. He was the one who had brought news of Derrick's father's death home, then proceeded to marry his mother five months later. And if you thought things could get any worse, he then proceeded to keep Derrick away from her when she had to go to the hospital after her accident. Derrick kind of hated Ernesto a lot. He honestly couldn't remember why his mom married the guy; then again . . . he didn't really care.

Derrick turned to Nathan, Ernesto's son, waiting for him to give them their jobs. Though he had started out as a really big jerk, Nathan had warmed up a little to Derrick. Whether he was sorry for Derrick or he wanted to do it for his step-mom, Derrick didn't know. But Derrick was glad to know that Nathan didn't hate him. He already had an abundance of enemies and didn't want or need anymore. He was glad that Nathan technically ran the theater now instead of Ernesto.

Nathan handed them each a list of the jobs. "Here are the jobs for today. You need to do all of these except for cleaning the ticket booth, concession stands, and fixing the lights. I already did those for you."

Derrick smiled, "Thanks."

Nathan smiled slightly, then frowned. "What are you three still doing here? Get to work!"

Rowley led the way back to the janitor's closet; which, with some help from Nathan, had been turned into a janitor's lounge. "Well, we have a lot of work to do! Let's get kickin'."

Derrick grabbed his janitor uniform and changed into it. "At least they bothered to wash them this week. Remind me to add that to this list of things I have to thank Nathan for." He grabbed a mop. "Okay, so first, we need to mop the stage." He filled a bucket of water and poured some soap into it.

Frankie got a mop and twirled it around, "Okay bro. But you are going to work on your acting."

Rowley nodded, "And if you try to get out of it, you're cleaning the bathrooms by yourself."

Derrick drooped his head, "Why do you guys put me through this . . . I am not very good at it . . ."

Rowley dropped the cleaning supplies he had been carrying. "What!? Did I just hear you say that?"

Frankie gave him such a look, "If I ever hear you say that again . . ." He growled. "Stop being so hard on yourself!"

Rowley put an encouraging paw on his shoulder. "You're a natural! It's in your blood, mate. Don't let anyone ever tell you different, you got it?"

Derrick sighed, then smiled a small smile. "Which play should we do?"

Frankie smiled, "That's our Derrick! Hmm . . . How about your favorite?"

Derrick's eyes widened, and he smiled. "Phantom!? Well then, what are we waiting for?"

So, they took their cleaning supplies up to the stage and got to work. Derrick started from the beginning lines of Phantom of the Opera and acted out the parts with his mop as he cleaned. Derrick didn't know why he loved Phantom of the Opera. He loved it because of its great story and interesting characters, and it had been a big part of his life. His parents had read it to him as a pup at night before he went to sleep. Almost every night, he would ask them to read it to him. He had gone to see the play in theater on his 10th birthday with his dad. And after his dad died, he had read the entire play to his mom while she grieved to help her feel better. He'd read it so much as a kid, he had it memorized to the second act by the time he was thirteen.

Frankie sat with the towel waiting for them to finish mopping so he could dry the floor and read the lines of all of the other characters. Then when it came time for him to dry, Rowley took a turn at reading the script. But Derrick didn't need the script. He'd memorized all the lines of his favorite character, The Phantom. They kept it up even while cleaning the bathroom, and by the time they were done with the script, they had finished every single job on the list.

When they gave the list of finished chores to Nathan, he gave them a surprised look. "You're done?" When they nodded, he went and checked all the stuff they did. When he came back, he had an impressed half smile on his face. "Well! I am impressed."

Rowley smiled. "Does this mean we can go?"

Nathan frowned, "No . . . My dad would have a fit if I let you three out early . . . But I can definitely let you just hang out here until your shift is done. I put a little . . ." He smiled a little. "surprise in the room for y'all."

The three friends looked at each other. A surprise? Nathan never did something like that.

Nathan frowned again, "If any of you tell Ernesto . . . I will never do it again."

Rowley went to the janitor's lounge and opened the door. A smell filled the air as the door opened, and they gasped when they saw . . .

"PIZZA!" They said excitedly.

Nathan chuckled as he watched them open the top box of pizza. "Y'know, you guys aren't so bad."

They smiled at him through mouthfuls of pizza.

Nathan rolled his eyes, "Don't tell anyone I said that either." He left the room in a hurry.

Rowley finished the pizza he had and turned to Frankie and Derrick. "'Ey! Let's take the pizza into the back room and eat while reading some of the old scripts."

Derrick smiled. "That's a great idea, my friend." He grabbed the boxes of pizza, "Let's go!

"Hey, listen to this line. I like it a lot." Rowley said, pulling the script he read closer.

Derrick and Frankie looked up, ready to listen.

Rowley cleared his throat and read, "Be not afraid of greatness. Some are born great, some achieve greatness, and some have greatness thrust upon 'em."

Derrick's eyes lit up, "Oh! I love that play. Twelfth Night by the master of playwriting himself, William Shakespeare. That is probably one of my favorite quotes!"

Rowley and Frankie traded looks, then looked back at their scripts.

Derrick quirked an eyebrow, "What?"

Rowley looked up from his screenplay with a look on his face, "So which one are you, Derrick?" Derrick rolled his eyes and turned away, but Rowley got up and followed him and got in his face. "Because I think you're great, Frankie thinks you're great, Cassidy thinks you're great, and even Elena thinks you're great." Rowley's ears perked up slightly, but then drooped back down.

Derrick put on an amused smile and tried to change this subject, "What's up with your ears . . . ?"

Frankie put his script down and came to stand next to Rowley. "Come on man! You say that's your favorite quote, but you don't think it applies to you! You let your worth be determined by what others think of you, but not the ones that really love you bro. Stop being an idiot!"

Derrick put his face in his paws. "I don't know why I torture myself. I can't seem to get that voice that tells me this crap out of my head. I used to act all of the time when I was a pup . . . but since Dad died and mom got hurt, whenever I tried to start acting again, Ernesto told me I was trash."

Rowley sat next to him and put an arm over his shoulder. "All you got to do is give it the boot, because you're the one that tells yourself that. Only you can stop it. You can start by not giving a darn what Ernesto thinks. Okay?"

Derrick sighed and put his face in his paws.

Ernesto came back at around 5:00 or 5:30, Derrick couldn't really tell from the clock in the janitor's lounge since the minute hand on the clock broke two years ago. He snatched the list from Frankie and thoroughly checked everything, against Nathan's protests. "Hmm . . ." he said walking back into the main room where the three were lined up in front of the concession stand. "You idiots have succeeded in impressing me. I'm impressed."

Rowley sighed in relief. "Thank you, sir."

Ernesto turned to him angry. "I didn't say you could talk, Aussie."

Rowley's face fell. "S-s-sorry, sir."

Ernesto gave him a look, "I didn't say you could apologize, either." He looked at all of them, "You did a good job today . . . Even though you forgot to bring the costumes to the drycleaners!"

Derrick put his paw up, "But Ernesto! That wasn't on this list!"

"He is right." Nathan nodded, "I know for sure that wasn't on the list. Why are you getting mad at them?"

Ernesto turned to Nathan. "Shut up. This is none of your business, son. Don't you have some papers to file or something?"

Nathan sighed, "Yes, sir . . ." He gave them an empty look and walked away.

Ernesto looked back at them and raised an envelope in his paw. "Here are your paychecks. You guys are allowed to leave." All three of them walked toward him to get their paychecks. He put his other paw up, "Except for Derrick. You two . . ." He pointed at Rowley and Frankie, "need to leave."

Frankie put his paw up, "Umm, sir . . . Can I stay? I need to be here so I can give Derrick a ride home."

Ernesto pointed to the door. "He won't be needing a ride, he can walk to your little shack. It's not that far . . ."

Frankie put his paws on his hips. "Yes, it is! It's ten miles from here. Are you . . ."

Ernesto glared at Frankie, "One. More. Word."

Frankie looked down in defeat. He turned to Derrick, "I guess I'll see you later dude . . ." He walked up to Ernesto and got his paycheck and left.

Rowley followed after giving Derrick a sad look.

Ernesto turned on Derrick. "I heard that you sassed my daughter."

Derrick didn't say a word or apologize, because he had no regrets about that. She deserved it.

Ernesto glanced at him again before taking a clipboard from Nathan. "No denial? Well then, if I didn't know better, I would say you were manning up. But we both know you're just a scared little pussycat on the inside."

Derrick glared at Ernesto but didn't say anything.

Ernesto smacked him. "Don't give me that look, dog." He watched Derrick compose himself after getting hit. "You are going to stay here and get all the clothes to the drycleaner and wait for them to be done, and then . . . you may walk to your friend's house. Nathan will give you your paycheck when you have finished." He turned to Nathan, "If he leaves before he is done. Call up Razor. Tell him I'll give him and his friends fifty bucks to beat the living tar out of Derrick." Ernesto gave Derrick one last glare and left.

Derrick rubbed his face, extremely angry . . . but honestly, he had become used to stuff like this. And that made him even angrier. He wanted to tear Ernesto apart, but he didn't because that would only make things worse for him. So, without another word, he went to where the costumes were and collected them to bring them to the dry cleaner.

After about three hours of waiting, the clothes were done. He brought the clothes back and hung them up and went to leave . . . and saw Nathan in the doorway. "What do you want?" He grumbled.

Nathan's face, though it showed no pity, showed something else . . . Derrick couldn't put his finger on it. But then Nathan handed him his paycheck. "I am sorry you had to go through that . . ." He then turned and walked away, letting Derrick leave.

Derrick frowned as he left the theater. He walked down the street, away from the theater. He sighed, what did he do to deserve this? He hadn't hurt anyone, but Ernesto treated him like a dirt clod instead of a living, breathing thing with emotions. He thought about his dad. He could remember only a few things about his dad.

Derrick thought back to the last time he had seen his dad. It had been his 10th birthday. He and his dad had gone to see the Phantom of the Opera as his birthday present. Derrick had enjoyed the time with his dad, and the play made the day even more memorable. After the play, they had gotten pizza when his dad told him that he had to go overseas.

Devon looked at his son, who smiled up at him as he ate a rather large piece of pizza. He had enjoyed spending the day with his son, but he knew he had to tell him. "Son . . ."

Derrick looked up at his dad. "Yeah, Dad?" He saw that his dad didn't look as happy as he should've been. He was worried. Did his dad not have fun today? He cocked his head, "Dad? What's wrong?"

Devon put his arm around his son's shoulders. "Son . . . I have to tell you something . . ."

Derrick looked up at his dad with a confused face. "What, Daddy?"

Devon sighed, "I have to leave for a while . . . I got a call from the army, and they need me overseas . . ."

Derrick looked at his dad, "Wait . . . You have to leave?" His eyes started watering up, "B-but what about us? You can't leave, Daddy."

Devon hugged his son, "I know, buddy, I don't want to go, but I am gonna be fighting for the safety of our country."

Derrick wiped his eyes and looked up at his dad. "L-like a hero?"

Devon smiled, "Yes, son. Like a hero. I am gonna be helping a bunch of people over there. But I'll be back in four years."

Derrick frowned, "B-b-but that's way too long . . . You would miss Christmas. And mommy's birthday."

Devon patted the boy's back. "It'll go by in a flash, and I'll be home before you know it. Okay?" He smiled at Derrick, "How about we go and get some ice cream after this?" He smirked and whispered, "Let's just keep that part a secret from your mom. You know how much she hates it when you eat ice cream."

Derrick's face lit up with a sad smile as he wiped the tears. "Really?" He hugged his dad. "I love you, Daddy."

A tear fell from his eye and trailed. "I love you, Daddy . . ." That day had been one of the best days of his life. His mind went to another memory, the day that he had gotten the news that his dad was dead. He had been practicing for a play he was going to be in when someone knocked on the door.

Derrick peeked around the corner and saw his mom talking to a jackal at the door.

June smiled when she saw Ernesto at the door, then it faded when she saw his uniform. "Ernesto . . . Come in, please."

Ernesto took off his hat and came into the house, "Thank you, June." He saw Derrick peeking out from the other room and gave him a look. "Unfortunately, I cannot stay long . . . I hate to have to be the one to say this, but . . ."

June put her paw to her mouth and breathed out a small gasp. "No . . ."

Ernesto frowned, "There was a surprise attack on the camp. Most of them died . . . Your husband . . ." He hesitated, as if he didn't want to finish the sentence.

June put her face in her paws. "No . . ." She cried.

Ernesto looked from June to Derrick, "I am sorry . . . I have to go . . . Take care of her." He quickly left the house and closed the door.

Derrick glared after him. What the heck did he mean by that? His dad couldn't be dead. His dad was the best soldier ever. Derrick walked to his mom. "He's gotta be lying, Mommy. Daddy can't be dead! He can't be. He promised he'd come back!"

June looked up at her son, tears in her eyes. "Oh, Derrick . . . He's gone." She pulled him into a hug.

"NO! He can't . . ." He cried into his mom's shoulder. "He can't be dead . . ."

Derrick kept walking, tears streaming down his face at the memory. If only his mom wasn't bedridden. If only his dad wasn't dead. If only . . . His expression turned angry. If only that punk Ernesto died instead of his dad.

A blasting car horn pulled him out of his thoughts. He looked around as a familiar truck pulled up next to him. "Get in, mate."

Derrick wiped his eyes, "Guys? Is that you?"

Frankie gave him a look, "Oh no, just two random people who just decided to drive by and pick you up, then leave you stranded in the middle of nowhere. OF COURSE, IT'S US! We weren't gonna let you walk all the way home."

Derrick smiled sadly and got in. "Thanks guys . . ."

Rowley noticed he had been crying and turned in his seat, "What happened? Were you cryin'? Did Jerknesto do something?"

Derrick shook his head, "No . . . He didn't do anything . . . I've just been thinking about my dad" He put his face in his paws. "Times like these are when I miss him . . ."

Rowley reached back and patted his knee. "I am sorry, mate. You've told me about your dad before . . . He sounded like an amazing wolf. He'd be proud of his son, no matter what his son thinks of himself."

Derrick began to cry again, "I miss him . . . So much . . ."

Rowley sighed, "I know you do . . . But you know what probably neva' would have happened if he was still alive? You neva' would have met us. We wouldn't even know each other . . ." Rowley smiled sadly as he passed a paper bag back to him. "And you never would have even tried chimichangas, which we got you two of."

Derrick wiped his eyes and took the bag. "Remind me to hug you when we get out of the truck."

Rowley laughed. "Mate, you probably won't need me too."

Chapter 3

D ERRICK SAT BORED OUT OF his mind in the radio station while Frankie played disc jockey in the sound booth, playing hits as the famous DJ, DJ K-Dawg. Derrick cringed because Frankie was in no way, shape, or form a dog. Besides, the name sounded so lame. But whenever he confronted Frankie about it, though . . . Well . . .

"Wow, Derrick." Frankie crossed his arms and glared at his friend. "That is extremely hateful and rude. The nickname is adorable!"

Derrick threw his paws up, "You're a leopard! NOT A DOG!"

Frankie stuck out his tongue. "It's a DJ name. It doesn't have to be accurate."

Derrick rolled his eyes just thinking about it.

The roadie, a golden retriever named Turner, carried a box out of the storage room, placed it on the table near the front door of the radio station, and opened it.

Derrick stood up and walked up behind him. "Hey, Turner."

Turner jumped and turned around, "OH! Derrick, didn't see you . . ." He composed himself. "Hi! How are you?"

Derrick smiled. "I'm good, buddy." He looked in the box and asked, "What's with all the leaves and stuff?"

Turner pulled some of the stuff out of the box. "Well, Frankie and his dad need someone to set up for the fall months. So, as I was taking inventory of all the stuff in the storage room, I found this box of fall décor and thought, why not?" He got up in a chair and tried to start hanging fall leaves around the room.

"That's cool. Here . . ." Derrick picked up some of the decorations and helped him hang them up. "Let me help you, Turner."

Turner chuckled, "Oh cool. Thank you, I really appreciate it."

Derrick smiled and helped him hang up some of the decorations. "So, how much do they pay you for this, again?"

Turner smiled, "I get five dollars an hour and work ten hours a week." He tacked a line of leaves on the border of the wall. "I am very happy with it. Not to mention I like hanging out with Frankie."

Derrick chuckled and put some fall window stickers on the window. "Frankie is a nice guy to hang out with."

Frankie walked out of the sound booth, "You bet he is."

Turner rolled his eyes, "Yeah, and he is humble, too." He said sarcastically.

Frankie smiled, "Yes, I am." He looked puffed up for a second, then he realized that Turner hadn't actually meant it. "HEY!"

Derrick smiled and patted his friend on the shoulder. "It's okay, buddy. We like you this way. If you change, we may not recognize you." He and Turner laughed.

Frankie smiled, but hid it because he was supposed to be angry. "Well then." He crossed his arms. "I guess you two don't want to go get some food with me." He walked to the door. "I had wanted to go get some burgers from Burger Binge. But if I am too humble, you probably don't want to do that with me."

Turner and Derrick traded glances, "WAIT! Burgers with Frankie sounds cool. Doesn't it, Derrick?" Turner chuckled nervously at the concept of not getting to eat burgers.

Derrick nodded. "Burgers are awesome." He stopped and started again, "I-I mean Frankie is awesome.'

Frankie feigned thinking about it, "Hmm . . . Are you guys sure that you wanna be with humble ol' me?"

Derrick and Turner looked at him with such a look. "YES," They said in unison.

Turner bit into his burger and got ketchup all over his face. "MMmmmm-Mmm Mmhmm" He said, trying to talk with his mouth full.

Frankie gave him a side glance. "Turner, actually chew and swallow your food."

Derrick gobbled into one of his burgers and finished both of them in under thirty seconds. "I love this place!" He took a sip of his chocolate shake.

Turner swallowed the burger he had been chewing, "I said thank you for bringing us here, man."

Frankie gave them both a look, "Darn canines! You guys are like monsters."

Turner stopped mid-bite and slowly traded glances with Derrick. "What did you just say?"

Derrick smirked and moved to block Frankie's way out of the bench. "I think he just insulted canines." He looked around. "Hey everyone!"

Frankie's eyes widened. "Wait . . . NO, DON'T YOU DARE."

One of the waiters, a wolf, came up, "Is there a reason you're disturbing the peace, sirs?" He said, glaring at Derrick and Frankie.

Turner got a mischievous glint in his eyes. "Yeah. This guy . . ." he pointed to Frankie.

Frankie's eyes went wide. "I TAKE IT BACK! CANINES ARE NOT MONSTERS!"

That turned every single canine's attention to Frankie, who tried to hide.

The waiter snarled, "Do you think that is funny, kitty cat?" The snarl made Frankie jump and yelp.

Derrick and Turner laughed so loud. "I don't think you should've said that out loud, Frankie."

Frankie slid under the table to avoid the glares.

One of the wolves at the counter let out a chuckle. "It's alright, guys . . . This is just one of those scaredy-cats."

All of the canines laughed, and there were a few shouts of "HEY!"

A German Shepard in the booth behind them chuckled, "Maybe you should make better friend choices."

Derrick turned to look at her and pulled Frankie out from under the table. "I am not going to go that far. Though he is not very bright, he's been my best friend for seven years, and if anyone wants to get at him, you have to go through me."

Frankie gave him a grateful smile. "Thanks bro . . ."

Derrick patted his buddy on the back. "You're welcome."

The other wolves and dogs started trading insults with their feline friends until an angry, young cheetah that Derrick recognized from high school as one of the nerdy writers, walked out of the kitchen in his trademark red hoodie and fedora. "ALRIGHT! IF I HEAR ONE MORE SPECIEST COMMENT FROM ANY OF YOU, I AM LEAVING!"

The wolf at the counter raised an eyebrow at the young cheetah, "Aaand just who are you supposed to be?"

The cheetah narrowed his eyes at the wolf, "My name's Vinnie, the grill-master, and if you want to keep getting the brisket I make for you every Wednesday, Frank, you'll watch your manners!" He gave them all one pointed look "Same goes for all of you. Not a word." He walked back into the kitchen.

Everyone looked at each other. As much as they wanted to carry on, the burgers they always bought from there were delicious. If the kid, the grill-master, left, there would be no more juicy meat. So, they kept their mouths shut.

Vinnie popped his head out the door again with a smirk, "Canines Rule!" He put his fist in the air.

The wolves and dogs opened their mouths in surprise, and the felines looked shocked, but he put his finger over his mouth. "Not a word about it." He smirked.

Everyone reluctantly went back to their conversations.

Frankie had a weird look on his face. "That was interesting. I should do things like that more often . . ."

Half the canines in the diner turned to glare at Frankie, including Derrick and Turner.

Frankie chuckled, "Uhhh . . . I mean . . . Umm" He looked down at his plate. "Burger."

They went outside after they were done with their food. Frankie had to go inside again to go to the bathroom. Turner volunteered to go with him to make sure that he didn't get beat up by vengeful wolves or dogs. Derrick decided to go wait near the truck for them when someone shoved him from behind. He stumbled a bit and turned around, seeing three figures behind him. "What?" A punch from the one in the middle landed him on the ground.

"There's no Cain here to help you this time, Hilman." A familiar voice mocked him.

"Razor?" He covered his face just in time to block a kick to his face.

"Yeah punk. It's me. I'm glad you recognized me. Now I can beat you unconscious, knowing you'll still be able to give me the credit!" Razor laughed.

Another kick hit him in the side, and he heard a devilish cackle of a hyena. Manny mocked him. "What's wrong little wolfy? Can't fight?"

Another voice, Buck's, laughed. "Hey, get him up."

His body was lifted from the ground, and Derrick looked forward through hazy vision. He saw Buck lean his head forward and charge. "UGH!" He said as the buck rammed into him with his antlers. He fell face first onto the ground.

"HEY." A gruff voice yelled.

Derrick heard the three guys whisper to each other and then run off, leaving Derrick in the dirt. His body hurt really badly. He groaned in pain as he tried to get up. A big pair of arms grabbed him gently and helped him stand. But Derrick's body couldn't take it, so he fell back down. He heard a frustrated grunt and two people yelling. He was picked up off the ground and placed in the back of a truck. And then everything went black.

Derrick heard his name being called. At first, it sounded like a blur of sounds, then it became clearer. "Derrick? Hey guys, he's coming around." He opened his eyes; at first, he could only see blurs, but as it cleared, he saw Cassidy and Rowley staring down at him.

Rowley saw he had woken up and helped him sit up. "Hey mate. Déjà vu or what?"

Derrick looked around, still very dizzy. "Where am I?"

Cassidy put a paw on his shoulder, "We're at Frankie's house. You're on your bed."

Derrick's eyes widened as he heard her voice, but he couldn't see because his vision was still a little hazy. He saw five blurs in the room in front of him, and one of them seemed to be much bigger than the others. "Why can't I see?' He asked.

Cain spoke up, "You were attacked by Razor and his cronies. They got a few good hits off you, but then I came along and scared 'em away. I put you in the back of Frankie's truck, we took the other kid home, then Frankie called these three."

Derrick's vision cleared up, and he saw his friends watching him worriedly. Cassidy and Rowley were by his bedside. Cain and Elena were leaning against the wall, and Frankie sat on his own bed. "Guys . . . ?" He suddenly registered who stood in front of him and jumped. "C-C-Cassidy?"

She smiled, "Hey, Derrick. Are you alright? Cain said you were attacked."

Frankie, Elena, and Cain had sneaky smirks on their faces, but they stayed quiet.

Derrick covered his face, embarrassed. "I-I think so . . . How long have I been out?" He rubbed his head.

Rowley shrugged, "We got here about an hour ago, but who's been keeping track? Not me."

Cassidy gave him a sympathetic look, "Do you need anything? Frankie made some coffee; do you want any?"

"Yeah." Derrick tried to get out of bed but winced, "Don't worry, I think I can . . ."

"Oh no, you don't, mate! You're stayin' in bed. You got a few bruises, and they are gonna hurt if you keep movin'." Rowley said, not letting him get off.

Cassidy smiled and gently patted him on the shoulder. "I'll go get you some." She walked out of the room and shut the door.

Everyone's eyes went to Derrick and just stared at him.

Derrick tried to play clueless, even though he knew what they were thinking. "What?"

Elena put her paws on her hips. "When are you going to ask her out!?"

Derrick's ears flattened but still tried playing dumb. "Ask who out?"

Rowley raised an eyebrow, Cain rolled his eyes, and Frankie threw a pillow at him. "YOU KNOW WHO WE MEAN." They yelled in unison.

Well . . . Rowley and Frankie yelled, Cain just said it in his normal voice.

Derrick chuckled. "Who . . . Cassidy? I don't know what you're talking about . . ."

Cain walked up to the foot of Derrick's bed. "Would you stop denying it? You two were made for each other. And if you do not ask her out before the school year is over, I will."

Derrick stared at Cain. "Wait . . . What?"

Cain walked back to the wall and glared at Derrick. "You have the perfect chance. There is a Christmas dance at the school, and you are going to ask her to it."

Derrick's eyes widened, and he shivered a little as Cassidy walked back in the room. "Here's some coffee, Derrick." She smiled, putting the cup on the dresser next to his bed. She looked at his face and noticed he was tense. "Are you okay?" She put a paw on his forehead. "You don't have a fever . . ."

Derrick chuckled, "Uh . . . It's probably just from the bruises."

Over by the wall, Cain gestured at him to get on with it.

Derrick froze up. He wanted to ask her so badly, but for some reason, he couldn't get the words out. He had to think of some way to ask her to go out . . . Then he had an idea. Mrs. Hatfield, earlier that day, had told the class that they needed to buddy up with someone and write a novel with them by the end of the year. Derrick had thought he would choose Rowley, but now . . . "Cassidy . . . ?"

She looked at him, "Yeah, Derrick?"

He took a sip of his coffee and put the cup back down. "You remember that English project . . . the one that we needed a buddy for?"

Cassidy smiled, "Yeah. I remember."

"How could she not? Wasn't it assigned this morning?" Elena muttered.

Cain nudged her lightly in the side and gave a sharp shake of his head.

Derrick reddened again. "Well . . . I wanted to know if you would like to be my partner."

Cain's eyes widened, as if impressed by Derrick's approach.

Cassidy smiled, "I'd love to, but I actually wanted to work with Elena."

Elena shook her head. "No. You go ahead and work with Derrick. I'll use the smart guy." She walked over and sat next to Rowley, putting an arm around him. "We'll be a good team!" She winked at the kangaroo, and his ears perked up.

Cassidy cocked her head, "Well then, I guess I can work with you, Derrick." She smiled.

Derrick beamed, "You will?" He tried to get out of bed and hug her, but the pain in his stomach made him wince. "Owwww."

Cassidy frowned. "Stop trying to move." She helped him lay back down and hugged him. He smiled and hugged her back. She let go and smiled, turning to Elena. "Come on. We have to go. My mom said she would save dinner for us."

Elena nodded and hugged Rowley, making his foot jerk and twitch, and got up. "See you later, partner." She walked out the door.

Cassidy rolled her eyes and gave Rowley a hug. "Sorry about that . . . She is like that a lot . . ." She smiled at the guys. "I'll see you guys at school." She waved and walked out the door. "Feel better, Derrick."

Derrick smiled as he watched her leave.

Cain smirked. "Well then! That's not quite what I expected when I said ask her out. But it's close enough!" He walked to the door. "Looks like I am done here. I'll see you kids at the game tomorrow." He gave them a nod and left.

Derrick slowly sat up on his bed. His stomach still hurt, but not as much. Rowley was still sitting on the edge of his bed, looking very nervous with his ears flat on his head. "Well . . . I actually asked the girl I like to hang with me . . . Now . . . I need to survive it without zoning out and staring at her like a complete idiot . . ."

Rowley patted his knee, "You're not the only one, mate . . ."

Derrick looked at him with raised eyebrows. "What?"

Frankie got off his bed and walked over to Rowley. "Don't worry about it, Derrick. I'll take care of Rowley's problem. Just focus on yours. Besides, I know who he likes." He led Rowley into the kitchen, leaving Derrick alone to think about his situation.

Derrick still had a smile on his face. He had just gotten a chance to spend more time with Cassidy. He sighed; he had never been this excited about English before. He sat up in his bed and started thinking of how he planned to tell her how he felt about her. "Oh boy . . . Derrick Hilman. You have a lot of work to do . . ." he mumbled.

Chapter 4

Derrick woke up before his alarm the next morning and reset it for 8 o'clock and let his friend get some extra sleep. He felt a lot better this morning. He took a shower, got dressed, ate breakfast, and made coffee. When he came back into the room, Frankie was still asleep. Derrick gave him a look and went to get his own pillow and smacked Frankie with it.

Frankie sat up. "What the heck?" He saw Derrick awake and up, and his jaw dropped. "Derrick? Are you even supposed to be up?" He got out of bed. "And what happened to your alarm?!"

All of a sudden, Derrick's alarm went off, and Derrick smirked. "I feel fine. So why would I not be up? Plus! I got a study date . . ." He smiled, then it disappeared. "Don't tell Cassidy I said that . . ."

Frankie rubbed his eyes. "What time is it . . ." He looked at the clock, and his eyes widened. "8 o'clock? I slept in? That has never happened before."

Derrick smiled and walked out of the room. "You're welcome. I made coffee, too, when you want it." He went into the kitchen and opened the fridge for some orange juice.

When he closed the door, Frankie stood there, standing where the fridge door was with his arms folded and a smirk on his face. "Does this happy attitude have anything to do with Cassidy?"

Derrick grinned and poured himself a glass of juice. "What makes you say that?" He asked, taking a sip from his cup.

Frankie got a mug from the cupboard and poured himself some coffee. "Because for one thing, you're up in the morning and happy WITHOUT YOUR PHANTOM MUSIC! And two . . . I heard you muttering a poem about her last night."

Derrick gave him a look. "I recited a poem in my sleep?" He shrugged. "Huh . . . I guess I am just talented." He took another sip of his orange juice.

Frankie smiled. "And another reason. You just called yourself talented. You literally never do that."

Derrick again smiled, brushing it away with a shrug. "I guess I just got motivated."

Frankie chuckled, "Yeah. By Cassidy." He ducked as Derrick playfully swatted at him. "Hey! Dude, I am proud of you. You are actually happy, you are getting the chance to hang with the girl you like." He downed the rest of his coffee. "Come on! Finish your orange juice. We have a big day ahead, and you have a study date."

Derrick smiled and downed the rest of his orange juice. "It's not a date!" He whined, but just thinking about it made him smile. He grabbed his book bag and went to get into the truck. This was the happiest he had been since that day with his dad. And what made him even happier was that Cassidy actually wanted to hang out with him and seemed excited about it, too.

Frankie got in and smiled. "Are you ready?"

Derrick chuckled. "Yes! Now hurry up and go before I start to get nervous."

Frankie smiled and put the keys into the ignition and turned the car on.

Derrick walked down the hallway with a smile on his face. As he walked down the hall, he passed Razor, Buck, Manny, and Lorena. Razor's face went from angry to confused and a little ticked off, Buck's mouth and eyes were wide, and Manny looked at him like he was from a different planet.

Lorena and her friends walked in front of him. "Whatever you're doing, it's doing something weird to your face."

Derrick gave her a smile, something he would never have thought he'd do in his life. "Well, Lorena, it is called a smile. Maybe if you used it sometime, you would actually have a boyfriend." He smiled and gently pushed her aside and kept walking.

Lorena turned around with her mouth wide and her eyes narrowed. "UUUGGGHHHH!" She turned and walked in the opposite direction in a rush.

Derrick walked into class and waved at Mrs. Hatfield. "Good Morning, Mrs. Hatfield."

Mrs. Hatfield looked up from her desk with a smile on her face. "Why hello, Derrick! You look like you are in a good mood today."

Derrick smiled and sat in his desk, "Oh, I just thought I'd smile today. It's really quite nice."

Mrs. Hatfield smiled. "Well I am glad that you decided to."

Rowley walked into the room with a smile on his face, "G'day mates! Got a big game today!"

Mrs. Hatfield smiled. "I can't wait to see you and the team take the field. I hope you guys win."

Rowley sat down in his desk. "With all the drills Cain's been putting us through, I am pretty hopeful." He looked at Derrick and did a double-take. "Derrick? You're smilin'! Where have you been keepin' that?" He slapped Derrick on the back. "I am glad to see you're so happy." He looked up at the door. "Cassidy! You broke him. I hear he hasn't stopped beaming all morning."

Derrick looked up and saw Cassidy, and his smile widened. "Hey, Cassidy!" He turned to Rowley with a smirk. "What makes you think she is the reason I am smiling?"

Cassidy laughed. "Oh, come on, Rowley! He's probably just in a good mood today." She came up to Derrick and gave him a hug. "It's nice to see you in such a good mood."

Derrick hugged back with a smile. "It's nice to see you, too."

Cassidy let go and went to her seat with a smile.

Rowley smiled and gave his friend a look, "Uh huh . . . Yeah. Just in a good mood today. Yeah right, mate! You're in love." He poked Derrick

Derrick just sat there smiling and calmed it down a little to a small smile. "Yeah . . . I am. I am really happy, I asked her out . . . on a study date. But it is a step closer to actually asking her on a real date!"

Rowley smiled at him. "That's the spirit, Derrick!"

Derrick nodded as everyone filed into the room, "So . . . You are doing your project with Elena?"

Rowley nodded, and Derrick noticed his ears perk up when he said Elena's name. "I almost told her no . . . But Frankie convinced me to just go with it."

Derrick smirked, "Oh, so I'm the one in love?" He patted his friend on the shoulder.

Rowley gave him a look. "Remember how I told Frankie if he tried to eat me, I would kick him? Same applies to you with this. Not. One. Word." His cheeks went super red.

Luckily, the teacher started the lesson, so the young kangaroo could not get any more red. The teacher taught them about predicates and sentences, and then they did a few exercises that helped them understand the subject better.

Then in the last fifteen minutes of the class, she stood up from her desk and told the kids to get with their chosen partners and start some work on the end of the year novel they would be working on.

Derrick got up and turned to go to where Cassidy sat, but got pushed to the ground by Razor.

Razor smiled at Cassidy. "Hey . . . So, do you want to be partners on this little project, Cassidy?" He winked at her.

Cassidy pushed him away. "Sorry loser. I already have plans." She went to where Derrick had fallen and helped him up with a smile. "I believe we have a novel to work on?"

Derrick smiled at her. "Sure!" He sat down, and she sat next to him. He watched as Rowley approached where Elena sat, shyly, only to get pulled down into the seat next to her and hugged.

Cassidy smiled as she watched them. "Those two are so adorable together."

Derrick looked at her. "Yeah, they are." He sighed internally and thought to himself, *"If only you thought that about us . . ."*

Cassidy straightened up and smiled. "Okay, so we need an idea for a novel. I was thinking we could do something, I don't know, maybe like a desert island romance or something like that." She looked up at him with a serious face. "What do you think about that?"

Derrick smiled at her. "Romance sounds amazing."

Cassidy chuckled. "Wow. It sounds really kind of creepy when you say it like that."

Derrick's eyes widened and put his paws up, "Wait . . . OH! I didn't mean for that to sound creepy. Did it really sound creepy?"

Cassidy laughed. "No. I am just messing with you. You look so cute when you're nervous."

Derrick's head shot up, "What?" Did she just call him cute?

"Nothing . . ." she looked away.

Derrick smiled. "So . . . about the project?"

Cassidy turned back and smiled, though still slightly red. "Oh, yes . . . About the project . . . So, I thought we could start with a group of friends that go on a pleasure ride on a friend's yacht, and . . ." The school bell rang, sounding the end of the class period, interrupting her train of thought. She frowned. "Aww . . . I didn't get to finish . . ."

Derrick put a paw on her shoulder. "It's okay . . . Maybe we could get together later and talk about it over some burgers . . . You know, if you want."

Cassidy gave him a wide-eyed look. "What? Derrick Hilman, are you asking me out on a date?"

Derrick's face reddened. "Oh . . . Umm . . . No. Wait. I mean yes . . . I mean . . ." He turned away, "Not that kind of date!"

Cassidy smiled, her face just as red, "Oh, so a study date?"

Derrick smiled. "Yeah. A study date. We can go to the Burger Binge after school."

Cassidy's eyes lit up. "Burger Binge? I loved that place! Is it really still around?"

Derrick nodded. "It hasn't moved." He started when he heard someone clear their throat and looked up. Frankie, Rowley, and Elena were looking at them with smirks on their faces.

"You two do know that class is over, right?" Frankie said, raising an eyebrow.

Elena chuckled. "You guys must have been deep in novel planning, eh?" She nudged Rowley, who chuckled.

However, Derrick noticed something odd. Though Rowley looked nervous, he didn't look as nervous as he usually got around girls . . . and he stood awfully close to Elena. He smiled a little when he noticed they were holding paws. "Sorry about that guys." He and Cassidy traded smiles. "Must have lost track of time.

Rowley dropped his spoon into his rice with a surprised expression. "You did WHAT?!"

Derrick smiled, "I know! I can't believe that I did it, either, but I did."

Frankie cut a piece of his chicken and ate it. "So, let me get this straight. You, the guy who passed out at the sight of the girl he has liked for six or seven years, actually asked her on a date? And she said yes?!"

He could feel his tail swishing behind him as he thought about it. "Well technically, it's a study date . . . But yeah."

Frankie and Rowley looked at each other, then back at Derrick. Rowley smiled, "You are on a roll, mate! First you ask her to be your project partner, and then you ask her on a date. What's next? Are you gonna propose?"

Derrick went tomato red at that and hid his face.

Frankie and Rowley looked at each other. "I think you hit something, Rowley." Frankie grinned and gave Derrick a look. "But I have to be the best man."

Derrick yelled a muffled, "Shut up!" from the inside of his hoodie. He popped his head out of the hoodie. "Oh . . . I need to borrow someone's car . . ." He said, looking sheepishly from Frankie to Rowley.

Frankie shook his head. "Nope. You are not using my truck. Can you even drive?"

Derrick nodded. "You took me for my license. Remember?"

Rowley finished his rice and licked his plate clean. "No worries, mate! You can use my car."

Derrick and Frankie looked at him in shock. "You're letting someone use 'Cherry Cola'?" Cherry Cola was the name Rowley had given his red Prius that he had gotten for his birthday.

Rowley smiled. "Yeah. Don't worry. I'll be there with you. So if you wreck it, I can just kill you and blame it on the wreck." He looked at Derrick's plate. "Are you gonna eat your cornbread?" Derrick and Frankie just stared at him, so he shrugged and took the cornbread. "I probably forgot to mention, Elena and I . . . are going to Burger Binge, too."

Derrick and Frankie just stared at him "When were you going to tell us that? That is awesome, Rowley!"

Rowley chuckled nervously. "Well . . . Umm . . ." He reddened. "She kinda asked me out . . ."

Derrick looked at Frankie, who had been at Rowley, then back toward Rowley. "When were you going to tell me you liked Elena?"

Rowley frowned as he ate the cornbread. "I'm sorry, Derrick . . . I should've told you, but liking a girl like Elena. I mean, that girl is kind of terrifying. But really amazing at the exact same time." He had a dreamy look on his face. He quickly snapped out of it, though, with a sheepish look. "And you had your own problem with Cassidy . . ."

Derrick hugged Rowley. "You're okay, buddy . . . It's okay. Just because I have my own problems doesn't mean I won't listen to yours.

Rowley smiled, "So . . . We can tag along on your little date?"

Derrick smiled. "Sure buddy, and then we can go to your football game and scream and yell like crazy when you take the field."

Cain nodded. "And if we don't win. I will work the team so hard, they won't be able to practice for a week." He chuckled. "I'll probably give you and some of the freshmen leeway because you guys are actually good at football."

Rowley smiled. "We'll meet you near the front of the school with Cherry Cola. And I may . . ." He narrowed his eyes at Derrick. "May just let you drive."

Cassidy sat at her table eating her chicken. Thinking about Derrick, of course. What else could she think about? Her best friend had asked her out. Granted, they were just going on a study date, but still . . . She smiled and took a deep breath and let it out. She broke off a piece of her cornbread.

Alex and Conner practically ran to the table and sat down across from her. "Is it true? Are you really going on a date?" They said in unison.

Cassidy chuckled. "Anyone ever tell you how creepy it sounds when you two talk at the same time like that?"

Alex gave her a smirk. "All the time!"

Conner chuckled. "They never stop. But you avoided the question: did someone ask you out?"

Cassidy smiled. "Well . . . Yes."

Alex smiled and gave her a high five. "Awesome!" He drew back his paw for a second. "You did say yes, right?"

Conner nudged him. "What else would she say? No? If a person asks you on a date and you say no, you are a moron."

Cassidy smiled. "Yeah. I said yes . . ." She smiled to herself. Connor had a point. How could she have said no to Derrick? He had actually asked her out, something she had been waiting for him do ever since she had gotten back from California. 'It's just a study date.' She kept telling herself that. But hey, maybe there is a real date in our future.

Elena sat down. "I agree. Any moron who would turn someone down when it comes to dating is not worth having. The only thing they will ever really get out of life is a black eye from me."

Cassidy turned to her friend. "So since you told them about me . . . I am gonna ask. What's going on between you and Rowley?" She smirked at her friend.

Conner gave Elena a look. "Rowley? From the football team?"

Elena smirked. "Yeah, the cute Aussie from the football team, we got a date today."

Cassidy spit out her orange juice. "He asked you out?!"

Elena sat up. "What? Oh no. You think that kid will ever work out the courage to ask someone out? When that someone is me? No way! I asked him."

Cassidy gave her a blank look. "I didn't even know that you even liked him."

Elena facepalmed. "How could you not know?! I've been flirting with him since we got back. I flirted with him before we left for Hollywood. I mean, you can't look at that boy and say he isn't adorable."

Alex gave Elena a confused look. "So wait . . . You asked him out? Is that even a thing? Girls asking guys out?"

Conner nodded and took a bite of his sandwich. "Of course! Haven't you ever watched movies? Happens all the time!"

Alex gave his friend a look. "I thought I already told you that movies are not all real stories. Just some stuff a script writer jots down on paper to get a lot of money."

Elena gave the two boys a look. "Anyway . . . Yeah, I asked him out. We're going to the Burger Binge." She gave Cassidy a smirk. "I couldn't let you and Derrick have all the fun."

Cassidy smiled. "That's awesome, Elena!"

Elena smiled, except it wasn't like her normal smirk. She had a genuine smile on her face.

Cassidy feigned a gasp. "Is my best friend turning soft because of a relationship?"

Elena glared at her. "No. I can still punch people, and my fist has the slight tugging on it right now. Watch yourself." She sighed, "If anyone is going to see me soft, it's Rowley. No one more. No one less."

Cassidy smiled. "That's actually sweet. I am so glad; the poor kid must have been shocked when you asked."

Elena chuckled. "Are you kidding me? The kid walked over for our little partner project thingee looking all nervous and stuff, and I just pulled him in the seat next to me and gave him a hug. And as he tried to start the project, I waited for him to actually say something. But he just bumbled along, so I randomly asked him if he wanted to go on a date. Well . . . When I did that, he gave me a surprised look and was like 'What?! B-b-but . . .' I just smiled at him as I watched him squirm. He probably didn't expect me to ask him at all. He finally nodded, and we started on the project."

Conner smiled. "He sounds like a nice guy. I am very happy for you. So, I guess that means you'll be coming to the football game?"

Elena smirked. "Oh yeah. I am ready to see Rowley and the team win. Mostly Rowley, though . . ."

Conner looked offended. "I'll be out there, too, you know. I'm the running-back." He smiled with pride.

Alex put a paw on his friend's shoulder. "Yeah. We probably should have mentioned that before."

Elena smiled. "Then that's two guys I get to root for." She reached to pat Conner on the head.

Cassidy nudged her. "Don't forget Cain. He is the quarterback and the coach, and he is gonna flatten the competition."

Alex chuckled. "As long as he doesn't flatten those bozos, first." He pointed toward Derrick's table, where Razor had stopped to bother Derrick and Cain had stood up, crossed his arms, and glared at Razor.

Razor looked like he thought he was going to die, and at that point, he was lucky he didn't. He turned and stumbled away, and Cain just sat down like nothing happened.

Cassidy shook her head. "I'll be surprised if those three make it to the game."

The rest of the school day went by extremely fast for Derrick. After his last class, he went to look for Cassidy and accidentally bumped into her on his way out of the classroom. "Oh. Hello. Sorry about that Cassidy . . ." He said, rubbing the back of his head with a nervous smile.

She chuckled nervously and backed out of the doorway to let him through, "No. It's my fault. I should've looked before coming into this room . . ." She chuckled nervously as they walked toward the front of the school. "So . . . I guess you heard that we're not gonna be alone, huh?"

Derrick chuckled. "Yep. I am happy for them, though. It seems like Rowley has had that crush for a long time."

Cassidy laughed. "Apparently, Elena has had one just as long." She smiled. "I think she's going a little soft."

Derrick laughed. "It's probably the opposite with Rowley! He's gotten a lot tougher. Elena is influencing him. He threatened to kill me if I crashed his car, then asked me if I wanted my cornbread"

Cassidy stopped, her eyes wide. "Wait, really? That doesn't sound like Rowley." She sighed and kept walking. "How did we miss it?"

Derrick looked down and thought to himself, *"Because my heart is focused on the most beautiful girl in the world right now, and there is nothing that can be able to distract me from her."* However, he didn't say it out loud; instead, he said, "I guess we were too wrapped up in our own lives to see it."

Cassidy nodded. "Yeah . . . I feel so bad, though . . . I mean, if she had told me . . . I could have helped her get him."

Derrick nodded. "Same here."

They neared the front of the school and saw Rowley and Elena talking near the Prius. Rowley didn't look the least bit nervous, which Derrick didn't see very often, and Elena was smiling nicely and laughing at something other than another person's embarrassment.

Cassidy's eyes went wide. "Well . . . That is new . . ."

Derrick did a double take. "Um . . . Rowley is actually having a conversation with a pretty girl! It's the end of the world."

Cassidy laughed. "I know, right?"

Rodney and Elena gave them a look. "What's so funny over there? Come on! We want to actually have time to eat, don't we?" Elena snapped, her smile going away.

Rowley smiled at her and threw the keys to Derrick. "Remember, mate. Trash it, and I kill you." He smiled and got into the back seat with Elena.

Derrick and Cassidy looked at each other with wide eyes. Derrick caught the keys. "Makes me feel so much better about driving."

Rowley smiled at him from the backseat of the Prius. "No worries mate! You'll do fine. I have complete faith in your drivin' capabilities."

Derrick shrugged. "Okay . . ." He opened the door for Cassidy, who smiled and got in the car. He got into the driver seat and turned the keys in the ignition. "Here goes nothing . . ."

They got to Burger Binge without getting into any wrecks, to Rowley's and Derrick's delight. They went inside, and Rowley and Elena went to their own table. Derrick and Cassidy slipped into one a few tables away.

A waiter, the same wolf from the other night, came up and smiled at Derrick. "Nice to see you came back after what your friend did. What can I get for you today?"

Cassidy facepalmed and whispered to Derrick. "What did Frankie do this time?"

Derrick chuckled. "I'll tell you later." He turned to the waiter. "We'll have two large Supremo' Burgeritos with chocolate shakes."

Cassidy's eyes lit up. "THOSE STILL EXIST?!"

The waiter chuckled. "Coming right up."

Cassidy turned to Derrick. "It feels so awesome to be back here! We used to come here all the time when we wanted to. I have some pretty good memories of this place." She smiled, looking around at everything.

Derrick smiled, but he kept his eyes on her. "Yeah . . . I do, too." He decided not to mention that almost all of them had to do with her.

Cassidy sighed and took out a folder. "So . . . About our project." She opened her folder. "I already told you about how it is going to be a desert isle romance where the kids are on a joy ride on their friend's boat. They get lost and drift for a few days and end up on an island. A lot of stuff happens, bringing the characters closer. The two main characters fall in love. And some hilarious scenes and dialogue happen somewhere in between all that." She sighed. "How does that sound?"

Derrick smiled. "I like it! So, where we start?" He looked in her folder and started pulling out one of the sheets. "Do we fill out one of these thingees?"

Cassidy smacked his paw. "No! Don't touch." She smiled. "Yes, that is the thing you fill out. But let me hand it to you so you don't accidentally mess up my organization!" She smiled and handed him the paper and a pen. "Now you can do it. Work on a guy main character. If you follow the sheet, you will have a good character." She smiled and got one of her own and started writing. "I found these online on the school computer. I printed out several copies to do several characters."

He looked at his paper for a second, very confused about what he should do. He looked up at Cassidy, and an idea formed in his head. He started writing his character and answering the character questions with a smile on his face.

After thirty minutes of writing, the two were interrupted by the waiter coming back with the Burgeritos. "Two Supremo' Burgeritos and two chocolate shakes for the lovely young couple."

Derrick and Cassidy's heads shot up, "OH! NO! We're not together." They said in unison.

Derrick sighed. Why did he say that? He really wanted to be with Cassidy.

The waiter just smiled a knowing smile and walked away. "Enjoy your food!"

Derrick looked at Cassidy and chuckled nervously. "Friendly service, huh . . ." He took a sip of his shake to hide his nerves.

Cassidy smiled, her ears flattened on her head. "Oh . . . Very friendly . . ." She tried to change the subject and saw Derrick's character sheet. She picked it up and read the name, "Brian Flagler . . ." She read through the description and smiled. "Good job! This sounds a little too much like you."

Derrick paled. "Am I not allowed to do that?"

Cassidy smiled. "No it's okay! I like it, you are really good at writing character sheets. Mine's name is Sara Kershaw. She is a little bit like me . . . except I am a husky, and she is a raccoon."

Derrick laughed, "Yeah, I didn't want to make Brian too much like me, so I made him with gold fur . . ."

Cassidy threw her head back and laughed, "Oh my goodness, that is perfect!" She looked at both of the characters. "Maybe we should use these as the main characters. You know, the ones who fall in love?"

Derrick smiled and nodded. "I couldn't agree with you more." He cringed at how creepy that sounded, but he looked up at Cassidy and saw she didn't even notice.

"Of course, these two characters are perfect for each other!" She smiled at Derrick. "I love the backstories, too. We could totally intertwine them, like making . . ."

She continued talking and explaining her storyline while Derrick sat and watched, his head in his arms. He loved it when she got focused like this. He thought the ways she planned things and her love of organization was kind of cute. He never tuned out a word she said because he liked her. He took a bite of his burgerito and just listened to her talk.

The waiter stood near the kitchen, the knowing smile still plastered on his face. "Hah! Not a couple, my tail. Look at those two and try to tell me there ain't something going on there."

Vinnie leaned out the kitchen window, his hat fixed on his head and a smirk fixed on his face. "Oh, there's definitely something going on over there, Willy." He laughed. "I sense L.O.V.E." They both chuckled and got back to work.

Cassidy and Derrick spent the next half hour talking about what elements would go great in their novel. Then Derrick looked at the clock. "Oh! It's been two hours! The game is in thirty minutes." He looked around for Elena and Rowley and saw them happily chatting at a table nearby. He walked up to the table. "Guys . . . The game is in thirty minutes."

Rowley stood up abruptly. "OH! We gotta go, Elena." Elena picked up her soda and walked toward the counter and took out some bills and placed them on the counter. Rowley's eyes widened. "You don't have to pay! I can pay."

Elena gave him a look. "But I am going to pay today."

Derrick just smiled and put his money on the counter before Cassidy could even get her paw into her purse. "I will pay today. You can get the next time."

Willy, the waiter, smiled, "'Cause there is totally gonna be a next time."

Derrick and Cassidy turned to the waiter. "What?"

Willy chuckled. "Oh, nothing . . ." He took the money and gave them their change. They turned to leave, but he stopped Derrick. "Hey kid."

Derrick turned as everyone else left. "Yeah?"

Willy nodded in Cassidy's direction as she walked to the Prius. "Good luck."

Derrick winced. "Um . . . Thanks. I definitely need it." He walked out the door and to the Prius.

Willy watched them leave and turned to Vinnie. "Yep, there is definitely something going on there." He smirked.

Vinnie laughed. "I assumed as much. The guy didn't stop staring at her."

Willy chuckled and smirked at his boss. "So, when you going to find someone, kid?"

Vinnie glared at Willy. "Get back to work."

Willy chuckled. "Of course . . ."

Derrick sat on the top row of the bleachers with Frankie, sipping on a lemon-lime soda and waiting for the game to start. "Who are we playing again?"

Frankie looked at the flier promoting the game. "Um . . . I think it's the Wolfglade Wolves."

Derrick heard the other side of the stadium roar with excitement and looked on the field. "Oh . . . No wonder they call themselves The Wolves . . . It looks like all of them are wolves . . . Oh, and a rat." He looked at the other team. "Wow . . . They are really serious about their school name . . ."

Frankie pointed at the field. "SEE, THIS IS WHY I THINK . . ."

Derrick put a paw over Frankie's mouth. "Don't. You remember how much trouble you got into last time. Do you really want an entire football team out to kill you?"

Frankie paled. "That would not be fun . . . I can't even outrun our football team! Imagine running from one with all wolves and a rat . . . They'd track me down and gut me before I reached the edge of town."

Derrick sighed. "You'd definitely be in some deep trouble." He stood up and cheered as the Tigers took the field. However, they didn't start playing yet. Instead, they heard a blast from a microphone, and a familiar voice blasted from the speakers.

"Hello everyone! It's me, Cassidy Wells." The field went nuts. She laughed and continued, "It's really awesome to see everyone here. Before the game, I wanted to come and tell you about a few things our schools are planning this year. First, of course, is the winter ball that our two schools join every year to have."

Both sides of the field erupted with cheers. Derrick didn't cheer because he never went to one of those things before. One, he didn't like events like that, and two . . . He didn't know how to dance. But still, he listened to her talk, and he felt happy. He looked around the field for her and saw her in the middle of the field.

"I am excited to share with you that the theme this year . . . is fictional characters!"

The field erupted again with cheers, hoots, and hollers. And this time, Derrick joined in. He loved fictional characters! "I really want to go to this now." He whispered to Frankie.

Frankie smiled at him. "You don't gotta ask me. Just go!" He said, clapping Derrick on the back.

Cassidy continued, "I hope to see every single one of your faces there." She paused, and Derrick had a feeling that she looked straight at him. "It'll be a blast. We're having DJ K-Dawg laying down some beats for your entertainment."

Derrick looked at Frankie who grinned. "Someone actually hired you?"

Frankie put his paws behind his head and put his feet on the seat in front of him. "What can I say? I got class."

At the same time, a tabby sat on Frankie's feet. "HEY! Do you mind?"

Frankie winked at her. "Sorry girl. Just gotta . . ."

Then he noticed the big tiger following her who glared at Frankie. "Are you flirting with my girl?"

Frankie paled and pulled his feet off the bench in front of him. "Oh no, not flirting . . . Why would I do that?" He chuckled nervously.

Derrick couldn't resist the opportunity to throw a little jab at his friend. "Because you do it all the time."

Frankie glared at Derrick. "Wow, thanks, best friend."

Derrick shushed him. "SHHH! Cassidy's talking again."

Cassidy's voice continued, "Okay, second. So, I have this big acting competition . . . and I have a problem. Literally no one has signed up. But I have more to tell, so don't get up and sign yourself up just yet. Let me tell you the stakes; there can be an unlimited amount of acts and actors, but the judges can only choose five of those acts. So, you're probably wondering what they are going to win . . ." Derrick could see her now. She stood in the middle of the field. "Well . . . There is this huge Fine Arts College in California called Clayson University of the Fine Arts. Any of you heard of that?"

A bunch of yells came from both sides. Derrick had wanted to go to Clayson since he was a kid! His mom and dad had brought him there and introduced him to all of his and his mom's professors, and they even let him act with the students. He missed times like that . . .

Cassidy continued, "There's a few of you . . . A few . . . How would you guys like a shot at going to Clayson, full scholarship? Because the top three acts will get that chance of a lifetime."

The cheers got even louder. Derrick's eyes were bugging. Here was the girl of his dreams, telling his school about an acting competition that, if they won, they could go to Clayson on FULL SCHOLARSHIP! He could have sworn that Cassidy's eyes had flicked upward towards him. Obvious that she saw this as a chance for him to redeem himself from last time. He thought back to that day. The last time he had seen her before she left . . . The day he let her down.

Thirteen-year-olds, Cassidy and Derrick, were sitting at the lunch table. Derrick was eating his sandwich and Cassidy her Oreos. She had just got done telling him about a huge acting show she had wanted to enter.

Derrick smiled at her. "Cass! That sounds like an awesome opportunity. You should do it."

Cassidy looked down at her Oreos and sighed. "I know it sounds cool . . . But I don't know if I am good enough to enter by myself." She put her head down on the table and sighed sadly.

Derrick scooted over a seat and put his arm around her. "It's okay, Cass. I have full faith in your acting abilities!" He hugged her. "You'll do great!"

Cassidy looked up at him with a grateful smile. "That's nice, Derrick . . . But I would feel better if I didn't have to do it alone."

Derrick smiled encouragingly. "You don't have to do it alone. You can find somebody who is willing to be your acting buddy."

Cassie brightened up. "That's a great idea." She looked at him, then down at the ground nervously. He could tell she wanted to ask something, but for some reason, she was shy. "What's wrong?"

"W-would you want to be my acting buddy?"

Derrick's expression turned sad. He remembered what Ernesto had told him when he caught him acting in front of the mirror. "What? You call that acting! You're a disgrace to your family! Your friends may say your good, but they are just being nice to you. It stinks, so you leave it to the pros." He sniffled, looking away. "I can't, Cassidy . . ."

Cassidy frowned. "Wait . . . Why not?"

Derrick put his face in his paws and cried. "I am a terrible actor . . ."

Cassidy hugged him. "Who told you that? I think you are amazing, Derrick! One of the best ever."

Derrick broke away. "No . . . I am not." He ran out of the lunch room crying, and everyone laughed.

A tear formed in his eyes. He had been too scared to face her after that episode, and he didn't see her again for four years as a consequence. But there she stood, back with another acting competition and another chance to perform for people, and another chance to get to her heart.

Derrick sighed; the football game had begun, but he didn't pay much attention. He did stand and cheer when Cain pulled a center sneak and let Rowley run with the ball and score a touchdown. He clapped when one of the younger guys in the defensive line intercepted the ball and scored a touchdown. He even clapped when Razor and Buck brought down the big quarterback at the last minute and let the Tigers win 32-30. But he didn't feel the excitement at all . . . Not one bit. He wanted to be in that acting competition . . . but he didn't feel like he would be good enough to enter. So, he pushed the thought out of his mind.

Derrick and Frankie made their way to the locker room to get Rowley so they could celebrate somehow. They saw the opening and were about to go inside when they heard someone run up behind them. "Derrick! Frankie! Wait up!"

Derrick turned to see Cassidy, Elena, and one of the freshman boys they were sitting with the other day. "Hey guys. Who's the otter?"

Cassidy's eyes widened. "OH! Umm . . . Alex. These are my friends, Derrick and Frankie. Derrick . . ." She gave Derrick a smile. "is the one I have been telling you about . . ."

Alex stuck his paw out. "Hi! Nice to finally meet you, Derrick."

Derrick smiled and shook the otter's paw, only to watch the otter get tackled by a blur. "AAAAALLLLLLLLLLLLLLLLLLLEEEEEEEEEEEEEEX XXXXXXXXXXXXXXXXXXX!"

"CONNER, WILL YOU GET OFF ME!" Alex yelled as the young wolf took off his helmet and got off. He quickly scooted out, holding his arm. "You know I bruise easily."

"Sorry, Alex . . ." He chuckled. "I was practicing my tackling skills . . ." He sighed and looked at Elena. "No one appreciates true talent anymore."

Alex got up and glared at his friend. "You're fixing to appreciate a punch in the face, my friend." He pointed at Derrick. "This is Derrick and Frankie." He smiled as Conner shook their paws. "Derrick is the one she's been telling us about."

Conner grinned and hugged Derrick.

Derrick looked a little surprised, but he patted the kid on the back. "Hi . . ."

Conner pulled away and turned to Cassidy. "I approve. He is really good for you."

Derrick and Cassidy exchanged wide-eyed looks. "What?!" They said in unison.

Rowley bounded out of the room. "Hey mates!"

Elena tackle hugged him, and he fell to the ground. "You did such an amazing job tonight! You are the best football player ever."

Rowley groaned and sat up and hugged Elena. "Thanks . . ." He looked at Frankie. "So that's how it feels to be tackled . . . Ughh . . ."

Derrick laughed. "Ouch . . . That looks painful." He looked at Cassidy and saw Razor coming up behind her. He opened his mouth to say something when someone pushed him, Frankie, and Conner, and they fell on the ground.

"Get outta the way losers!" Razor said, leering at them. He looked at Cassidy and smiled. "Hey, Cassidy. Did you like what you saw out there and come to congratulate me?"

Derrick's stomach lurched. This guy was beyond disgusting when he smiled. He looked like one of those guys who were so good looking, it made every other guy sick.

Cassidy looked at her friends on the ground and then back at Razor. "No. I could honestly care less about you. I came to see Conner, Rowley, and Cain." She tried to get out of Razor's grasp, but he just tightened it.

"Aw, come on, princess. I know you like me. Now come on. Show me how you feel." He smirked.

Cassidy smirked back. "Okay . . . If you insist!" She brought her knee up and kneed him in the crotch, causing him to groan in pain and let go. She chuckled at him and pushed him to the ground. "I learned that one from Elena!" She turned to Buck and Manny, who were watching with wide eyes. "You boys want a piece of me, too?" She put her fists up.

Manny and Buck shook their head so fast, if they weren't attached to their bodies, they would have rolled away. "No. No way, Cassidy! Please . . . Don't hurt us."

Cassidy feigned sadness, "Fine . . . You guys twisted my leg." She pointed to Razor with a smile. "Could you two just take care of him for me, please?"

Buck smiled. "Of course! Thank you for not killing us!" He and Manny picked up Razor and carried him away.

Cassidy turned to the others. "You know, I have a feeling those two would have girlfriends if they didn't hang out with Razor. They are actually kind of nice."

Elena smiled and high-fived her. "That was awesome, girl! You're learning from the master!"

Cain watched from the doorway. "Nice hit. Saved me the trouble of kicking their butts.

Derrick smiled at her. "That was amazing! I-I . . ."

Cassidy smiled. "I know . . . I don't really use it unless I need to . . ."

Rowley smiled and grabbed Elena's paw. "So, what are we doing just sittin' around, chattin'? Don't we have some celebratin' to do?"

Cassidy traded glances with Elena and the two boys. "You mind if we join you?"

Derrick and Rowley turned to Frankie and gave him their best sad eyes. "Please, Frankie?"

Frankie almost said that girls and freshmen weren't allowed, but Cain glared at him. "Uh . . . Sure. They can come."

Cain's glare softened a little, and his lips quirked into a smirk.

Elena and Rowley exchanged a hug. "YES!"

Alex and Conner high-fived and hugged Frankie. "THANK YOU SO MUCH, FRANKIE!, YOU WILL NEVER EVER REGRET THIS FOR THE REST OF YOUR LIFE!"

Cassidy smiled and stood with Derrick and watched them. "Just like old times, right . . ."

Derrick looked at her. "Yeah . . . Like old times . . . Except this time, I am going to be there for you when you need me."

Cassidy looked at him, and her eyes softened. "I have never blamed you for leaving . . . I knew what you were going through." She whispered as the others talked about what they were going to do that night

Derrick hugged her. "I am so sorry . . . I should've been there and performed with you, regardless of what Ernesto thought of me . . . I am glad you're back, though . . ."

Cassidy smiled. "I am, too . . ."

They spent the night at Frankie's watching movies and playing video games and eating up all the snacks. They all had a blast, and by 3 o'clock in the morning, only Rowley, Derrick, and Cain were awake.

Derrick smiled as he looked at all of his friends sleeping on the couch. Alex snoozed on the floor curled up with one of Frankie's blankets, and Conner slept on the one person couch with a pillow. Frankie had gone into his own room to go to sleep instead of on the couch with several sleeping people. He smiled at Cassidy who was leaning on him with a pillow and sleeping. Elena was doing the same thing on Rowley's shoulder, except without the pillow.

Derrick watched as Cain and Rowley tried to beat each other at the wrestling game, and surprisingly, Cain was losing. He glared at the remote, trying to figure out the controls while Rowley ended up wiping the floor with his fighter. "Darn controller." Cain growled when he got beat for the fifth time. He looked at Derrick, "Hey lover boy. You take a turn." He passed the controlled to Rowley, who gave it to Derrick. However, as Derrick took the controller, Cassidy woke up.

She picked her head up from the pillow and rubbed her eyes. "I am sorry, guys . . . Didn't mean to fall asleep."

Derrick smiled and took his arm from around her. "It's okay. Almost everyone else did, so you have nothing to worry about."

Cassidy smiled tiredly. "Oh yeah . . . Okay then." She realized she leaned on Derrick and sat up abruptly. "OH! Sorry. I didn't mean to fall asleep on you . . ."

Derrick shrugged. "I didn't mind . . . You were asleep, and I didn't want to wake you up." He smiled at her.

She chuckled. "Well . . . I am up and awake now. So, I might as well just play. If I am allowed . . ." She smiled.

Derrick handed her the controller. "Here you go! Knock 'em out."

Rowley gave her a terrified, wide-eyed look, "No . . . Oh gosh . . ."

Cassidy smiled. "Oh yes. You're toast, Manchester."

Derrick chuckled as she did exactly what she said she would do and ended up winning not once, but three times.

Rowley crossed his arms as the word 'Winner' flashed across Cassidy's screen. "How did you get so good?"

Cassidy stretched and winked. "Life over there got boring real fast sometimes. A girl's gotta have a hobby, right? I actually got into video games one night when I came back home from a show. My roommate was playing an old MMORPG game, and since I couldn't sleep, I asked to join her. That led to other types of gaming systems, and now I can play almost every single one. It took years of practice, though."

Derrick watched her talk and listened to her as she told Rowley about her video game endeavors. She was so smart and talented, almost like the perfect girl. He cringed a bit at how sappy he was being, but he knew he was right.

Chapter 5

DERRICK FROWNED AS HE SWEPT the stage by himself. It had been a few weeks since the fun game night, and he hadn't talked to Cassidy in weeks outside of school. Ernesto had been giving them, as in Rowley, himself, and Frankie, extra jobs and separated them from each other. Derrick had all the jobs that had to do with cleaning the stage and theater area.

He sighed and kept sweeping the stage. It was his last job of the day, but he needed to finish the work. He finished sweeping and put the dust from the dustpan into the garbage, then put the broom and dustpan away.

He went through the list again to make sure he had completed everything. Ernesto would get terribly mad, even if he found one grain of dust on the ground. Once he had made sure he had done everything correctly, he turned his list in to Nathan.

Nathan smiled. "You've been doing good work . . . You can go ahead and have free time."

Derrick nodded and walked back into the main theater and backstage. He just sat there not doing anything, not even thinking. He looked at the costumes, then back at the floor. Then he looked at the costumes again, and he smiled sneakily. He walked over to the costumes and took the Phantom of the Opera costume out and changed into it.

He walked up to the mirror and smiled, posing. He put his mask on and fiddled with it until it looked like it did on the movie poster. He stared into the mirror and quoted the Phantom of the Opera in a strong voice. "Blood! . . . Blood! . . . That's a good thing! A ghost who bleeds is less dangerous!" He heard voices outside and went to the curtain and peeked out.

His eyes widened when he saw Cassidy and Nathan talking. He put his ear to the opening so he could catch their conversation. Nathan said, "It is an honor to have you here, and an even bigger honor that you want to use the theater as the place for holding your competition."

Cassidy grinned. "Oh, it's really nothing. This theater just has such good memories..."

Nathan smiled at her. "Well, I am going to let you scope the place out... I have some paperwork I need to do before Ernesto gets back in two hours." He left.

Derrick watched as Cassidy walked toward the stage, occasionally stopping to put her paw on one of the chairs. She looked extremely happy from what he could tell. Then again... theaters are supposed to have that effect on people.

He watched as she climbed on the stage and admired the curtains. He realized that if he didn't move, he would be caught, so he moved away from the curtains. Unfortunately, Cassidy saw it and came closer to where he stood behind the curtains. "Who's there?"

He had no idea what to do... He couldn't let her find out it was him, so he disguised his voice. "Does it matter?" He said in a much deeper voice.

Cassidy walked closer to the curtain. "Of course, it does! Everything matters." She drew back the curtain and gasped. "The Phantom!"

Derrick smiled at this and, for the fun of it, quoted one of his favorite lines from Phantom. "If I am the phantom, it is because man's hatred has made me so. If I am to be saved, it is because your love redeems me."

Cassidy smiled at him. "I see you have studied up on your scripts." She closed the curtain and just looked at him. "You look quite familiar... Do you go to school at Tigerthorn?"

Derrick scowled. "Perhaps..." he said. "Perhaps I don't go to school... I am the Phantom, after all." He beat himself internally. He shouldn't be doing this. This was not going to work.

Cassidy gave him a look. "Perhaps... But I'd say that you are probably more an intriguing person than a Phantom."

Derrick smirked and started walking toward center stage, "Oh? And what makes you say that, my dear girl."

Cassidy chuckled. "The real Phantom is a little taller than you are."

Derrick made a face. "You dare mock me?" Derrick narrowed his eyes; she was telling him Phantom facts? She had no idea how much that offended him.

Cassidy smirked. "Oh... I dare."

Derrick glared at her long and hard. "Hmmm... I have taken a liking to you, miss... Perhaps we shall meet again soon?"

Cassidy smiled. "I would like it, if we did. You are very mysterious... but familiar in some ways."

Derrick heard someone come into the main theater. "I must go . . ."

"Miss Wells? I have finished my paperwork. Are you in here?"

"I'll be out in a second!" She yelled to Nathan. Turning back to Derrick, she smiled, "How about you meet me at the Winter Ball?"

Derrick sighed. "I shall be there, my dear."

Cassidy turned back to the auditorium but looked once more at Derrick, only to find that he had sneaked away.

Derrick quickly changed out of his costume. What had he been thinking, playing the Phantom? Now he had a date at the ball with the girl he liked . . . AS THE PHANTOM OF THE FREAKING OPERA. He put his regular clothes back on. He had no idea how he would explain this to the guys . . . In fact, he was more comfortable not telling them. But he knew he had to do it at some point. He frowned and stared in the mirror at himself. On the other hand, it was nice to actually act again. He hadn't been able to do that freely in a long time . . . He smiled at his reflection and walked out of the dressing room.

He quietly hung the costume back up, and walked into the Janitor's lounge without anyone noticing. Rowley and Frankie were in there, cleaning up the supplies for the day.

Rowley stood up as he walked in. "DERRICK! Where the hell have you been? We had to tidy up without you, and Nathan said you were the first one finished."

Frankie nodded. "Yeah man! You better not have been playing dress up again."

Then they got a good look at Derrick's face, which had become slightly pale. Rowley gave him a look. "What happened to you, mate?" He pulled a chair out for him and helped him sit down.

"Y-You guys will not believe what just happened . . ." He stuttered to them. He told them how he had finished his jobs early, so he decided to mess around in the Phantom costume. He told them about how Cassidy had come in and caught him in it, and how he acted like the Phantom so she wouldn't know it was really him under the mask. And then he got to the part where she wanted to meet him at the dance. "So . . . That is what happened . . ."

Rowley and Frankie just stared at him. Rowley facepalmed, "Dude, you flirted with the girl of your dreams as someone else, and now she wants to meet that someone else at the dance. Mate . . . You have a problem."

Frankie gave Rowley a look. "It doesn't sound that bad . . . I mean, he could go to the dance, have some chit-chat with Cassidy and then whip off his mask to reveal the handsome devil underneath!"

Derrick paled a little. He'd have to take his mask off in front of Cassidy.

He couldn't even tell her how he felt about her, and now he had to tell her how he had dressed up as the Phantom and flirted with her? He didn't think he would be able to do it.

Frankie shook his head after thinking it through. "No, that wouldn't work at all . . ."

Rowley shrugged, "There is an easy way out of this . . ." He turned to Derrick, "You're not gonna like it, though." He sighed, "All you have to do is tell her. Telling her will make everything a lot less hard."

Derrick nodded. "Yeah . . . I think that's a . . ."

The door opened, and Cassidy stared in. "Oops, this isn't the . . ." She saw Derrick and the other two. "GUYS!" She came in and hugged them. "Oh wow . . . I have really missed you guys. We haven't talked in a while. How are you guys doing?"

Derrick froze; now was his chance to tell her. But instead, he said, "H-Hey Cassidy. We're doing great."

Cassidy put her paws on her hips, her smile getting brighter, "What are you boys doing here?"

Derrick chuckled "Well . . . we work here . . ." He chuckled nervously. "Did we forget to tell you?"

Rowley shook his head and sighed, and Frankie facepalmed.

Cassidy smiled, not paying any attention to the other two. "Yeah . . . I believe you did forget. But it's okay. I am not mad; I actually think it's cool that you work as janitors in the theater. You get access to all the scripts and the costumes."

Derrick saw a glint in her eye and wondered if she knew that the Phantom had been him, but then she grinned and hugged him. "Well, I got to go . . ." She paused for a minute, then extended her paw. "Can I see your phone?"

Derrick took his phone out of his pocket and handed it to her. "Here you go! Why do you need it?"

"I am putting in my phone number so you can reach me about meeting up again about our group project, or if you want to hang out or just talk." She handed the phone back and gave Derrick her phone. "Put your number in mine." He took the phone and put his number in, trying hard not to shake. Cassidy smiled and took her phone back. "See you boys later!" She waved and left the Janitor's lounge.

Derrick smiled and sighed. He turned back to Frankie and Rowley. "I got her phone number!" He hugged the phone, "Now I can talk to her when I need her."

Rowley and Frankie crossed their arms and stared at him. "What happened to telling her?"

Derrick winced, "Aw . . . Well, I . . ."

Rowley shook his head. "No excuses. We are just going to have to find another way to fix this . . ."

Derrick shrugged. "I don't know . . . Maybe we should just let me go through it. I mean, I got to act for real for the first time in years, and it felt amazing, and she bought it! Maybe it's not a bad idea to keep it up."

Frankie and Rowley exchanged glances. "Well . . ." Frankie said, "If it gets you to not treat yourself like a terrible person, it should be worth a shot."

Rowley nodded reluctantly. "Okay. I agree . . . but you have to actually tell her at some point. Otherwise, this is just a waste of time."

Derrick smiled at them. "I will do my best . . ." He turned to the door. "I just gotta find some way to get Nathan to let me borrow the costume . . ."

Nathan gave Derrick a weird look. "You want to borrow the Phantom costume? For a dance?"

Derrick nodded. "Uh . . . Yeah?" He chuckled nervously. "It probably sounds really, really weird, but it's a little bit hard to explain . . ." He just rambled on and on.

Nathan smirked. "It's for a girl, isn't it?" he interrupted.

Derrick stopped rambling and looked down. "Yes . . ."

Nathan chuckled. "I don't have a problem with that."

Derrick's head shot up, and he grinned, "Thanks! Remind me to add this to the list of things I will never be able to repay you for." He ran back to the Janitor's lounge.

Nathan looked confused and yelled after him, "Wait. There's still room on that list?" He chuckled, going back to his work.

Ernesto looked at them all lined up. "You bozos did an okay job today . . . You can all go." He handed them their paychecks.

Derrick and the other two turned to go, but Ernesto stopped him. "Hey, Derrick. I wanna talk to you . . ." He looked at Rowley and Frankie and said, "Don't worry, you two. I ain't making him walk again!" He turned back to Derrick. "Lorena's been complaining up a storm about how you have gotten such a nice attitude. Honestly, I could care less about Lorena's little pet peeves. I like a worker with a good attitude. However, she also says you've been hanging with Cassidy Wells, that actress girl. Is that true?"

Derrick nodded. "She's been a friend of mine for a while . . . And we also are working on a project for English class."

Ernesto nodded. "Hmmm . . . Okay. English projects are good . . . As long as that is all that's going on. I am definitely not opposed to having friends . . . but if you are looking for a relationship, I wouldn't go for her."

Derrick cocked his head. "Why not, sir?"

Ernesto sighed. "Well . . . You are a janitor. She is a movie star. Those two really don't ever mix unless it's a fairy tale. And last I checked, this is reality,

Derrick. Don't pursue her . . . You're only going to get your heart torn up."

Derrick turned to leave. "Like you actually care . . ."

Ernesto shrugged and called after him. "I could just let Razor tear you up instead! Much less harmful than a heartbreak."

Derrick froze, his paws clenching into fists. "Shut up, sir." He walked out the theater door and to his friends.

Rowley looked at him with a worried look, "What did he say this time?"

Derrick got in the back of the truck. "Nothing . . . I don't want to talk about it."

Rowley and Frankie traded looks, and Rowley got into the back seat next to him. "Which is it, Derrick? Is it really nothin', or do you just not want to talk about it?"

Derrick looked at Rowley. "I honestly would rather not talk about it."

Rowley put a hand on his friend's shoulder. "Are you sure? Because we're your friends . . . If anyone should be good at listening, it is us."

Derrick frowned. "It's just Ernesto is pretending to care about me, when all he really wants is to make me miserable. He told me to stop trying to hang out with Cassidy. He said she and I are only a possibility in fairy tales and that I should wake up to real life."

Rowley hugged Derrick. "Well, who cares what Ernesto thinks? Derrick, if Cassidy is going to like you, it's going to be in the here and now. Have you seen the way she is around you? If that is not proof she likes you, I don't know what is. Ernesto and his opinions can go to hell for all I care!"

Derrick smiled a little. "Thanks, Rowley . . . I feel a little bit better."

Rowley smiled. "Come on then, mate. How about we go and get some dinner before everythin' closes. That'll get your mind off your troubles!"

Derrick smiled. "Food would be amazing right now . . ."

Frankie smiled and turned on the truck. "Your wish is my command!" He laughed maniacally as the car roared to life.

Rowley gave Frankie a look. "Don't do that, mate. That's just creepy."

Chapter 6

THE NEXT DAY, DERRICK WALKED through the hallways of the school glumly. He passed by all the students as if they weren't even there.

Lorena tried to get in his way. "Hey! Janitor boy! Why you look so sad? You finally realize what a waste of space you are?"

Derrick just sighed and walked around her. He didn't have time to listen to her today. He felt a little too glum to humor her.

Lorena didn't like him ignoring her at all. "HEY! Wolfy! I'm talking to you." She put a paw on his shoulder to make him turn around, only to get it shrugged off.

Derrick didn't need her ridicules; he wasn't going to hear them today. He just kept walking, ignoring everyone else.

Razor and his cronies walked up to him and completely blocked his way. "What's your problem, little puppy? Are you sad? Are you gonna cry?" They chuckled as he just stood there, staring blankly at them. Their laughter died down as he didn't say a word. "Um . . . Hilman?" Razor shook the guy by his shoulders but didn't get a response.

Manny gave Razor a scared look. "Maybe he is sick or something . . ."

Razor looked at Derrick and shook him again, looking a little worried. "Hilman? Are you okay, man? Do you need to see a doctor?"

Derrick's blank look didn't go away. "I need to get to class. Can you move?"

Razor looked at him, his expression going from worried to amused. "Oh, so you are really just brooding. That doesn't scare me kid. I . . ."

Derrick punched him in the stomach, interrupting his sentence. "I don't have time for crap like you today, Razor." He stepped over Razor and continued to class.

Derrick walked into the classroom and slumped down into his desk. Mrs. Hatfield looked up from her desk. "Derrick? Are you alright?" Her eyes widened. "You aren't going to pass out again, are you?" she asked nervously.

Derrick smiled a small smile and chuckled dryly. "No . . . I am okay, just a little bit tired." He put his head down on the desk and hoped that the teacher didn't ask him anymore questions.

She didn't, to his relief; she just watched him with slightly worried eyes, but went back to her notes after a while.

Rowley walked in and sat in his desk. He shot a worried look at Derrick. "Y'okay mate?" He put a paw on Derrick's back and shook him slightly.

Derrick lifted his head and smiled slightly. "I am fine, buddy. Just a little tired."

Rowley sighed with relief. "Oh good, I thought you had gotten beaten up or sick or somethin'. I saw Razor lyin' in the middle of the hallway talking about a darn wolf. I guess Cain had to punch him again . . ."

Derrick chuckled and sat up. "Oh no. I did that. He got in my way, trying to be all dark and menacing, so I punched him in the stomach."

Rowley's eyes widened. "Really? Well . . . That could get you into slight trouble . . ."

Derrick sighed. "Oh, I am counting on that. But I am surprisingly not bothered. I don't care what they think of me. I ain't gonna let them in my head, either."

Rowley smiled. "That's good! Although the punch may have been a little unnecessary, if you ask me."

Derrick nodded in agreement. "Yeah, probably . . . So was the dejected look. I probably should just smile . . . I mean, they already think a lot of stuff about me. Why not add crazy to the list?"

Rowley chuckled. "Oh, you already have plenty of that, mate!"

Derrick playfully shoved his friend. "Oh, do I? At least I am not as crazy as Frankie."

He heard Frankie's voice come from the back of the room. "I am right here! I can hear you talkin' junk."

He turned to say something snappy but saw that Frankie was talking to a girl . . . who just happened to be the cheetah that he had made uncomfortable the first day of school. He turned back around and hit his head on his desk.

"You okay, Derrick?" A voice chuckled.

Derrick looked up and saw that Cassidy had walked into the room and now stood near his desk, looking down at him with smile. He smiled at her tiredly. "I am okay . . . Just a little tired. I didn't sleep very well last night . . ."

Cassidy sat down at the empty desk next to him and looked at him with a confused look in her eye. "Why couldn't you sleep? Were you sick?"

Derrick smiled as he remembered the reason he hadn't slept. He had been thinking about Cassidy. But of course, he couldn't say "I have been thinking about you." That would be really creepy. So instead, he lied. "It's not that I wasn't trying . . . It's just someone . . ." He raised his voice so Frankie could hear, "doesn't know how to stop snoring!"

Frankie heard this and shouted, "HEY! It's a medical condition. I am taking medicine for it . . ."

Cassidy frowned. "Derrick! You shouldn't make fun of Frankie and his medical conditions. You ought to be ashamed of yourself."

Derrick put his head down and looked very sad. "I didn't mean to make fun of him . . . I am just really tired."

Cassidy lightened her expression and rubbed his head. "I am sorry . . . I didn't mean to get mad . . . You're tired . . . I'll let you rest." She patted him once more on the head and walked to her seat in the back of the room.

Derrick smiled and sighed. She had patted him on the head! He liked being patted on the head, especially when she did the patting.

Rowley gave him a sneaky smile. "You enjoy that, Derrick?"

Derrick glared at him. "When's the last time you got something like that?"

Mrs. Hatfield stood up and welcomed the class, and they dived into their lesson for the day. "Okay! So today, we're going to learn about punctuation and when to use it." She taught her lesson for the day and then went through several exercises with them.

Derrick worked on the problems one by one and had almost finished when he his phone buzzed in his pocket. He looked at the teacher, who sat at her desk working on grading papers. He took his cell phone out of his pocket and looked at it. It was a text . . . FROM CASSIDY! His eyes widened as he read the text. "Hi ;)"

He turned to look at Cassidy. She smiled and waved, then pointed at the phone. He looked back at his phone and read. "Oooh, texting in class . . . You are a rebel . . . I like it! Anyway . . . Just texting to ask if you wanna meet during lunch or after school to talk about our project more."

Derrick smiled and texted back, "OF COURSE! I'd love to."

Cassidy texted back a smirk-y face, "Someone is eager to hang out. Your tail is wagging like crazy."

Derrick turned around and looked at his tail, which wagged back and forth. His ears flattened in embarrassment, and he texted back. "Yeah . . . It does that at very weird times."

Cassidy texted him back. "LOL ;) I am sure . . . So yes?"

Derrick smiled and texted back. "Yes. :)"

Derrick walked toward the lunchroom for lunch when someone ran up beside him.

"Derrick!" Cassidy said. "Glad I caught you . . . I wanted to tell you that we can meet during lunch and work on our thing. Elena said she'll sit at the other table . . . but we'll have to do our work with Alex and Conner watching."

Derrick smiled. "It's okay! Those kids are really nice. I really don't mind sitting with them."

Cassidy smiled. "Good. Come on, then." She offered him her paw which he took, and she led him to get food. Then they went to sit at the table.

Conner and Alex were already there. Conner making fun of Alex by waving his steak in his face. "Look, Alex! Steeeeeeeaaaaakkk! You want some?" He laughed and snatched it away. "Oh wait! I forgot . . . you eat leaves."

Alex glared at him and held up his fork. "Yeah . . . I don't eat meat, but I may make an exception for you."

Conner laughed. "Aw yeah, right! Like you would eat me." He chuckled, but Alex's expression didn't change. Conner's smile disappeared. "Alex, you are kidding, right . . ."

Alex gave him an evil grin. "Do you really want to find out?" He snapped his jaws, making the young wolf jump.

Conner scooted closer to Derrick and grabbed his arm. "Don't let the evil, wolf-eating otter get me! If he kills me, he gets all of my video games!"

Alex smirked. "You're such a scaredy-wolf! I would never eat up my best friend." He scooted towards Conner and gave him a hug.

Conner, however, thought that Alex was attacking him and yelled. "Oh no! 'Tis the end of me!" He patted Alex on the head. "Farewell, my good friend. You may devour me now . . ." He closed his eyes and cringed.

Alex let go and scooted back to his seat, mumbling, "Such a drama queen."

Conner let go of Derrick's arm and scooted back toward where he had been sitting. "Hey! I am not a drama queen!"

Derrick smiled. "He's a good actor . . ."

Cassidy smiled back as he watched them fight. "Yeah! He wants to go into the acting competition, but he is too young. But in the next two or three."

Derrick smiled. "Yes! I hope to be here when he wins."

Cassidy's smile disappeared. "Wait what? Aren't you going to enter? It's an amazing opportunity, especially an opportunity to go to a good college! Don't you want that?"

Derrick smiled sadly. "Of course, I do! I just am still . . . conflicted."

Cassidy shrugged. "Well hopefully, you change your mind in the next few months. I'd really like to see you enter the competition!"

Derrick smiled slightly. "I will definitely think about it long and hard." He pulled her folder from where she kept it. "Time for planning?"

Cassidy smiled and tried to get it back. "Come on! Don't mess with that folder."

Derrick laughed. "Oh? You mean this folder?" He waved it around.

Cassidy snatched it from him with a grin. "Give me that!" She chuckled and took out the papers. "Let's get to planning then."

They spent the rest of lunchtime talking and planning the ideas for their novel, with the occasional interruption from Alex and Conner. But of course, they couldn't finish their planning at lunch, even without the interruptions of the two younger guys. So, they decided to meet after school at an ice cream shop a few blocks away from the school.

Derrick went through the rest of his classes with anticipation. Every time he got the chance to hang out with Cassidy, she made his heart beat even faster. This time was no different. He felt like whenever they were together, his life meant something bigger than it had before.

He finished his school work fast, and when class finished, he scrambled out the door and went looking for Cassidy.

He found her sitting by the flagpole with her paws on her lap. She stood by the flagpole waiting for him. He walked out of the school crowd and up to her. "Hey, Cassidy!"

She looked up. "Hello! I was beginning to wonder if you were still coming!"

Derrick smiled. "You know when I say I am going to be here for you, I meant it. I am not going to intentionally desert you. Or . . . in this case, since we're going to get ice cream . . . Dessert?" He giggles

Cassidy laughed and looked up at him, her ears twitching. "That's very sweet . . ." She chuckled at her own pun. "I am glad to have you as a . . ." She paused for a second. "Friend." She smiled.

Derrick smiled when he heard the little pause. He offered her his paw. "Ice cream?"

Cassidy smiled as he pulled her up. "Ice cream."

They walked away from the school and towards the ice cream. Cassidy looked at him. "So . . ." She swung her arm around as they walked and held paws. Derrick had loosened his grip so if she had wanted to let go, she would. But to his delight, she hadn't. "I'd really like to hang out with you more . . . like this" She looked down at their paws. "Like old times. Where we'd go racing down the streets, setting off doorbells, and then running away as fast as we could."

Derrick smiled. "Those were good times . . . I've missed those times."

Cassidy smiled. "Well, so have I . . . That's part of the reason I came back. I missed the times we've had together."

Derrick smiled and, as they approached the ice cream shop, opened the door. They walked into the ice cream shop, and memories of their twelve-year-old selves flowed into his mind in little flashes. He saw them walking into the shop together and buy the same type of ice cream. Then Cassidy would jokingly take her finger and take some of his ice cream with a smirk and a laugh. Then he would do the same. Then they'd sit down and talk about everything and nothing for hours until the shop owner literally had to carry them out of the shop.

Cassidy walked up to the counter and looked at the flavors. "Wow! They sure have a lot of new flavors."

Derrick stood next her. "Hmm . . . Yeah. They made an effort to get as many new flavors on their menu as possible. Honestly, the s'mores is my favorite . . . But I think you'll lean more toward that one." He pointed at the Triple Chocolate M&M's ice cream.

Cassidy's eyes widened. "I can't believe that they still have this one! I love Chocolate M&M." They ordered their ice cream and sat down. Cassidy smirked and dipped her finger into Derrick's ice cream. "Hmm . . . Yep, I think I like S'mores too."

Derrick feigned shock, even though he knew that she was going to do that. "Oh, do you?" He did the same thing to her ice cream and smiled. "Two can always play that game."

Cassidy smiled. "So . . . Would you rather work on a project that we have till the end of the year to finish . . . or would you like to just hang out and talk?"

Derrick chuckled and pretended to think about it. "Hmm . . . Well . . . I wouldn't want to get bored." He winked at her.

She hit him in the arm. "HEY!" She chuckled.

Derrick smiled and put his head down and looked at her. "I'd love to just hang out with you."

Cassidy smiled. "Oh! Good. I got worried that you were actually going to want to work on a project instead of talk to me." She smirked. "Then I would have to find a new friend."

Derrick frowned, and his ear fell flat on his head. "You would really find a new friend if I just wanted to work on our project? Wow . . ."

Cassidy reached over the table and patted his head. "You don't need to worry about that . . . I am not thinking of changing friends anytime soon . . ."

Derrick smiled. "That's a relief . . ." He started eating his ice cream. "You know . . . Pistachio ice cream is one of the best I have ever had." He turned to look at the counter. "Maybe I should get a pint to eat at home . . ." He shook his head, turning around. "No . . . Then Frankie would take it as revenge for stealing his pop tarts."

Cassidy feigned shock. "You stole his pop tarts?" She shook his finger at him, "Oh, you bad boy." She chuckled. "Yeah . . . That probably would be a terrible idea . . ." She hesitated for a second, like she wanted to tell him something.

Derrick cocked his head. "What's on your mind?" he asked.

Cassidy shrugged. "Oh . . . Well . . ." She paused, ears drooping a little, and her tail wagging. "There's this guy I met . . ."

Derrick's eyes widened. She liked a guy . . . She just told him that she liked another guy . . . But he didn't want to be rude, so he gave her a grin. "Really? Tell me about him?"

Cassidy smiled sheepishly and giggled. "He is tall . . . He loves the theater, as far as I can tell; he is a nut about it." She prodded her head on her paw. "He has an amazing voice that just gives me chills whenever I hear it, and . . . he is a gentleman, from what I can tell."

Derrick's eyes widened. She had fallen in love with him! But not him, him; but the him that had dressed up as the Phantom. He sighed, feeling his heart shatter into a million little pieces "He sounds amazing." He said smiling at her, trying very hard to hide his disappointment.

Cassidy scooped up the remains of her ice cream. "Yeah . . . The only problem is . . . I have no idea how to tell him how I feel." She looked up, "What would you say to the person you liked?"

Derrick's heart leapt. This was his chance to tell her how he felt. "W-Well . . . I would say something l-like this . . ." He looked at Cassidy and smiled, "I-I like you, Cassidy . . ."

Cassidy cocked her head, looking slightly confused. "It's that easy?"

Derrick's heart fell. She had mistaken his confession of affection for his advice . . . He sighed, "No, Cassidy . . . More like simple. It's never easy to tell someone you like them . . ."

Cassidy nodded. "Okay . . . When do you suggest that I tell him?"

Derrick sighed. "Just tell him . . . Tell him at the dance. That'll be the best place."

Cassidy nodded. "Okay . . ." She gave him a look. "So about the dance . . . Are you going?"

Derrick frowned. He actually did plan on going . . . as the Phantom, not as Derrick. "No . . . I have stuff I need to do . . . I wish I could go, though. I'd love to meet the guy you like . . ." And punch him in the face for being an idiot and not telling her how he felt himself . . . But of course, he didn't say that out loud. That would've been rude and inconsiderate.

Cassidy smiled at him. "Don't worry, I am pretty sure you know him."

Derrick just nodded. "Yeah . . ." He wasn't really listening to her, though. He was a little bit sad that she said she liked another guy that wasn't him, even though . . . he technically was the other.

His phone buzzed in his pocket. He looked at it and saw that it was from the hospital. "She wants to see you."

He stood up abruptly. "I have to go . . ."

Cassidy looked at him. "What? Did I say something?"

Derrick shook his head. "Not you at all . . . My mom wants to see me." He smiled and offered her his paw. Even though she had just passed him up for himself, he still didn't want to go back on his promise to always be there. "You can come with me, if you want."

She beamed. "Oh. Really? I wouldn't want to impose . . ."

Derrick shook his head. "Nonsense! My mom really likes you, and she'd be delighted to see you again."

Cassidy smiled and took his paw. "Okay. I'll come."

Derrick helped her up and waved to the guy behind the counter. "Thanks for the ice cream." He opened the door for her. "After you." He said with a wink.

She smiled. "Why, thank you, my good sir." She patted him on the shoulder and walked out the door.

Derrick opened the door to his mom's room. "Mom?"

June put the book she read down and smiled at him. "Derrick! Thanks for coming."

Derrick beamed and came over to hug his mom. "Why wouldn't I come? You're my mom. I actually kind of like you."

June chuckled and hugged him back. "You better, kiddo. I gave birth to you."

Derrick chuckled and motioned for Cassidy to come in. "I brought a friend with me. You remember Cassidy? You've met her before, she had left town a little bit after the accident."

June saw Cassidy and got a mischievous twinkle in her eye. "Of course, I remember her, Derrick."

Derrick's eyes widened, and he shook his head like 'NO, MOM. DON'T DO IT.'

Cassidy smiled at June and shook her paw. "Nice to finally see you again, Mrs. Hilman."

June smiled, "Please, call me June. Derrick told me you came back; he still thinks highly of you."

Derrick stood behind Cassidy, his fur standing up and shaking his head rapidly.

Cassidy smiled. "Well, of course, he does! We've been friends for five years. I would hope he had the decency to tell you about me." She chuckled.

June grinned at Derrick's embarrassment. "Yes, my little guy has good choices of friends." She winked at Cassidy. "You keep an eye on him. He is trouble sometimes."

Derrick groaned. "Mooooooom! Not in front of Cassidy."

Cassidy turned around and slugged him on the arm. "Come on, Derrick . . . Your mom and I are having fun." She turned back to June. "Do you have any embarrassing stories about Derrick from when he was younger?"

Derrick gave a sharp shake of his head, even though he knew his mom wasn't going to listen to him.

June gave him a gleeful look. "I am his mom! Of course, I have some funny stories about him." She snickered, "Oh! There was this one time he was five . . ."

Derrick's eyes widened at the mention of a five-year-old him. He did NOT want his mom mentioning that. He coughed. "Mom, you said you wanted to see me?"

June smiled at him. "Yes." She turned to Cassidy. "Don't worry . . . We will get a chance to embarrass him with funny stories and picture albums later." She looked at Derrick, "Um . . . OH! I wanted to celebrate your dad's birthday with you . . . You do remember, right?"

Derrick couldn't have ever forgotten. He had remembered his dad's birthday since his dad went to war and had remembered since. "I remember . . ."

Cassidy frowned at the mention of Derrick's dad. "I never met him . . . But Derrick told me a lot about him. He sounded like an amazing guy."

June nodded, wiping her eyes. "He was a great guy . . . He shouldn't have gone overseas. I knew that it wasn't a good idea, but I let him. Always keep telling myself he made the right choice in going . . . But I didn't like it." She started crying.

Derrick sat by his mother's bed and held her hand. "It's okay, Mom . . ." He said, about ready to cry himself. "Don't blame yourself . . . That will not bring him back . . ."

Cassidy watched and hugged Derrick, trying to comfort him as he comforted his mom. Derrick smiled up at her. "Thank you for coming . . ."

June wiped her eyes and watched them with a smile. "Would you like to join us, Cassidy? We're gonna have cake and watch a movie . . ."

Derrick, who still hadn't stopped hugging Cassidy, looked at her. "Please? It would be fun if you stayed."

Cassidy smiled. "Of course, I'll stay. That sounds like fun!" She gave Derrick a look, "But first . . . Can you let me go?"

Derrick realized he was still hugging Cassidy and smiled sheepishly. "Oops, sorry . . ." He let go and giggled nervously.

She turned around and left the room for a second. "I'll be right back."

Derrick waved as she left. He turned back to his mom, who gave him the look only a mother could give. "What?! Did I do something wrong again?"

His mom crossed her arms. "Derrick Matthew Hilman. Have you asked that girl out on a date yet?" Derrick's pulse quickened as he tried to think of a creative lie, but she kept going, "I didn't think so." She smiled at him. "That girl is perfect for you! You like her, and I can tell you that she likes you back."

Derrick frowned. "But mom . . ."

June kept on talking. "Did I ever tell you how I met your dad?"

Derrick put his face in his paws. "Yes. Yes, you have."

June chuckled and went ahead and started telling the story. "Your father and I were almost like best friends in high school, but back then, I had a major crush on him, and vice-versa. So, this one day, our friends took us to this abandoned theater, the same one that we own today, and they locked me and Devon in there alone. The whole thing was so silly, to be honest."

Devon rattled the doors, trying to get out. "DANGIT!" he said, turning to June. "They locked us in! The rascals!"

June chuckled. "Mom did warn me I hung with a shady crowd."

Devon laughed. "I think I know who the masterminds were. They must have teamed up to get us here." He growled a little.

June sighed and turned to look around. "Yeah . . . But at least they locked us in a theater. I love theaters!

Devon smiled and walked up to where one of the old Broadway posters hung. "Yeah! Every time I go into a theater, I feel . . ."

"Like you never want to leave?" June asked, finishing his sentence.

"Yeah!" Devon said, turning to look at her.

She smiled, gazing into his eyes. He could feel his face heating up and his tail wagging behind him, but he didn't look away

His eyes suddenly lit up. "Hey, you know how this theater was into doing big productions?"

June nodded. "Yeah, I used to come here as a kid and watch them. I even got to play a part in a few of them." She gave him a confused look. "Why?"

Devon grinned. "Well . . . they had a back room with copies of all the scripts of all the plays they have ever done."

June's eyes sparkled as she remembered. "Oh yeah! I used to love to sit in there and read the scripts during breaks!" She gasped. "Do you think it's still here?"

Devon shrugged. "Let's go find out!" He said, taking her paw and leading her through the broken-down theater to the back room.

The back room, though very dusty, was still filled with shelves and shelves of old screenplays and scripts.

June's eyes lit up as she stepped towards one of the shelves, with Devon following behind her, and pulled out one of the scripts. "Look, Devon! It's Hamlet!" She opened the script and thumbed through it.

Devon looked over her shoulder and watched as she flipped through the pages of the script. "It's in pretty good shape for being locked in an abandoned theater for five years."

June sighed. "I just wish someone would rebuild this theater . . ." She looked around at all the ruin with a frown. "This used to be such a beautiful place."

Devon smiled. "It still is!" He squeezed her paw, which he was still holding.

She looked at the ground, trying to hide the emotions she felt for Devon. "June..."

She looked back up at him and saw he was fidgeting. "Devon?"

He smiled and chuckled. "I am sorry... I must look so silly right now. I definitely feel silly..."

June cocked her head. "Wait what?!"

Devon sighed. "June... I am in love with you... And I feel so silly because I've always been too chicken to tell you."

June's eyes went wide. "Y-You... You do?" Devin nodded, and she smiled. "Well... Devon... there is actually something I..." She was interrupted when Devon leaned in and kissed her. She froze; the guy she'd been crushing on for most of her life was kissing her.

Devon's eyes were squeezed shut. He kissed the girl of his dreams! He had finally told her how he felt, and now he was kissing her... He almost fainted when she kissed back.

June pulled away after a few minutes, her whiskers slicked back.

Devon had a smile on his face. "You were saying?" He chuckled, caressing her face.

She smiled. "I-I think you already know..."

Devon grinned. "So... This a good enough first date for you?"

June stood there, looking into his eyes. "Well, there is one thing that would make this night better." She reached into one of the book shelves, pulled out one of the plays, and showed it to Devon. "Could you read this to me?"

Devon looked at the title of the play and smiled. "The Phantom of the Opera." He pulled her close to him. "Another excellent choice!"

June sighed and smiled. "He read to me until we both fell asleep. When our friends came back for us, they found us sitting on the stage, asleep."

Derrick smiled a little. "I forgot how much I loved hearing that..."

June rubbed the top of his head. "So, go make your own story! You obviously like this girl."

Derrick sighed. "But Mom, she told me she likes someone already..."

June sighed. "Then give her a reason to want you!" She put a paw on his shoulder. "Son, you're an amazing kid, and I love you very much. I also know what's best for you. That girl makes you light up like Christmas whenever she talks to you. This girl is the one, I can tell!" Derrick stammered, trying to come up with something. June put her paw up. "No. I am your mother. I like that girl and hope to see her as a daughter-in-law soon."

"MOM!" He sputtered.

She smirked. "I am serious." She quieted down as the door opened and Cassidy walked back into the room.

Cassidy smiled. "Sorry I took so long. There was someone in the bathroom." She stopped when she saw Derrick's face and smirked. "Hmm . . . I am guessing you brought up something that he didn't want you to?" She chuckled when he gave her a look. "Your nose was twitching."

June smirked at her son. "You could say that . . ." She chuckled.

Derrick's fur stood on end, and he tried to find something to change the subject. "So . . . where is the cake?"

June scratched her chin. "Hmm . . . It should be here by now." She pressed the call button. "Hey, Carissa? Is the cake almost here?"

"Yes, ma'am! It just passed the desk right now, and it looks good. I hope you and your kids enjoy."

June smiled and pressed the button again. "Thank you, Carissa. Oh, and the boy is my son. The girl is his girlfriend."

Cassidy and Derrick looked at each other and then back at June, "OH. No no no! We are not a couple." They said in unison.

Carissa chuckled through the speaker. "Okay. Well, enjoy it anyway."

The door opened, and a dragon in blue scrubs carried in a covered cake. "Here you go, ma'am. Funfetti cake with chocolate icing." He opened the cake and looked up at June. "If I may ask, Mrs. Claw, what is the occasion?"

June sighed. "Sure . . . I don't mind, Chet. It's my late husband's birthday today . . . and I want to celebrate it with cake and a movie." She gave him a look. "And Chet? How many times do I have to tell you to call me June?"

Chet smiled. "Sorry, June . . . Oh! When is he going to get here? Should I wait with the cake?"

June frowned. "Oh . . . no. He isn't coming. He passed a few years ago. That's why I said late."

"Oh! I am sorry . . . I didn't mean to . . ."

June waved it aside. "It don't matter . . ." She wiped a tear. "He wouldn't have wanted us to spend his birthday like this."

Chet smiled. "Well, I got to go, Mrs. Hilman, before I get fired."

June waved him off. "Well then, get on. I'll see you later." She chuckled as Chet left the room, "That boy has some funny stories about medical school." She looked at Derrick. "I may even adopt him." She laughed. "You always did want a dragon, right?"

Derrick chuckled, remembering a childhood dream. "Yeah, I did . . ." He looked at the cake hungrily. "So, are we going to eat that or just sit here and stare at it? Because I am hungry!"

After they had finished hanging out with June, Derrick walked Cassidy back to her house.

She smiled at him. "Well . . . Thanks for the awesome day, Derrick . . . I had a really good time." She gave him a shy smile. She hugged him and turned to go into her house. She turned around, "Are you sure you aren't coming to the dance? I think you would enjoy it . . ."

Derrick frowned. "I am sorry, Cass . . . I don't think I can make it . . ."

She walked back toward him and put a paw on his shoulder. "Don't feel bad. I am not gonna force you to do something." She smiled. "You have a week to think about it if you want to change your mind." She waved and walked into her house.

Derrick sighed as he watched her go. He really, really liked her. If he hadn't have been going to the dance already as the Phantom, he would've told her he would be there. But no . . . He had promised her he would be there as the Phantom . . .

He sat down on the curb and called Rowley. "Hey, Rowley?"

He heard Rowley's tired voice on the other end of the line. "Derrick? Whadya want . . . it's 9:30 at night . . ." He growled. "This had better be good."

Derrick rolled his eyes. "You sound like whiny cat!"

Rowley sighed. "I am hanging up in three, two, and . . ."

Derrick shouted. "OKAY! I got to spend the day with Cassidy today . . ." His face heated.

He heard a loud yelp and a bump from the other side of his phone. "YOU DID WHAT?! That is awesome! I am so proud of you, bro. Now, all you gotta do is tell her."

Derrick sighed. "Slight problem with that . . ." He went on and told him about how she had told him she was interested in another guy, and how she had asked his advice on how to tell him that she liked him. He also told him about how he had manned up and told her . . . only to have his confession of love taken as a suggestion of how she could tell her guy how she felt about him.

Rowley stayed quiet for a while as he listened to Derrick pour out his frustration over the day's happenings before he finally said something. "Wow man . . . That sounds terrible. Any idea who the other guy is?"

"It's me . . . As the Phantom." He sighed. "But with my luck, I am glad it didn't end up being one of those Wolfgladers." He balled a paw into a fist. "Those wolves and their big muscles and their heavy lifting . . . Probably think they are better than everyone . . ."

As he said this, two teenage wolves pulled up in a Chevy and rolled down the window. One of them poked his head out the window. "Hey, kid! You lost? Need a ride?"

Derrick smiled and put his paw over the receiver. "Hi! Sure, a ride would be cool!" He went back to talking to Rowley. "I was also gonna ask you to drive me home, but I just met two guys who are willing to give me ride."

Rowley mumbled gratefully. "Does that mean I can go to sleep?"

"Yes." Derrick chuckled. "By the way, did you fall out of your bed?"

Rowley yelled through the phone. "I will kill you if you don't let me go back to sleep ..."

Derrick chuckled. "Goodnight, Rowley." He hung up the phone and walked to the waiting car. "Can you guys take me to 2751 Morning Lane?"

The driver, a slightly brighter white than Derrick himself, nodded. "Sure! It's only a little bit out of our way. Hop in the back!" He jerked a thumb over his shoulder toward the back seat.

Derrick smiled and got into the back of the van. "Thanks for stopping by. If you hadn't offered a ride, I would've gotten picked up by an angry kangaroo, instead.

The wolf in the front seat chuckled. "Don't know any kangaroos, but that doesn't sound fun."

The guy next to the driver chuckled. "If you think that's bad, you should meet our friend Paul. He sleeps with a gun under his pillow. It scares the living daylights out of everyone. Though he says it's for protection ... I think he just does it to scare people. No one ever wakes him up unless they are in another room."

Derrick shivered. "That is kinda spooky ... Is he a wolf?"

The driver shook his head. "Nope, He is a rat. Everyone always assumes he's a wolf when we talk about him. Never figured out why ..." He stopped at a stop sign and turned to face Derrick. "Do you mind if we make a stop before we get you to where you need to be? We need to pick Paul up for an outing we planned for tonight, and we are running a little bit late."

Derrick nodded. "I am good with that. I ain't in a rush."

The driver smiled and started driving again. "Awesome." He suddenly hit his head with his paw. "Where are my manners? Sorry ... I have a random kid in my car, and we don't even know each other's names yet! I'm Raul, and this guy over here ..." He jerked a thumb at the guy next to him. "Is my brother Lowe."

Lowe turned around with a smile and shook his paw. "Hi!"

Derrick shook Lowe's paw with a smile. "Nice to meet you two! I'm Derrick."

Raul smiled at him in the rearview mirror. "Nice to meet you, too, Derrick." He narrowed his eyes at Derrick. "I've never seen you around before ... Where do you go to school?"

Derrick smiled. "Oh, I go to Tigerthorn!"

"Is that place as cool as I've seen and heard?" Lowe asked with a curious look.

Derrick scowled. "I wouldn't be the one to ask ... I don't have very many friends there. Just a handful."

Raul sighed. "That sounds hard, bro. But the school itself is okay?"

Derrick nodded. "Oh yeah! The school is great, and the teachers are amazing . . ." He sighed. "I heard Wolfglade is awesome . . ."

Lowe chuckled. "Is that so? It sounded like you weren't too impressed by their . . ." He chuckled. "Big muscles and heavy lifting."

Raul gave his brother a side glance and chuckled. "And the fact that they're better than everyone else."

Derrick coughed. "Um . . . I may have said that out of jealousy . . ."

They pulled up in front of a house, and a rat came out and got into the car. "Hey guys. Who's ready to PARTY?" He pumped his fist, and then he saw Derrick. "Who's this guy?"

Derrick recognized him as one of the guys on the Wolfglade football team. "Hey! I recognize you . . . You're from Wolfglade!"

The rat nodded. "Um . . . Yeah. And obviously, you are not."

Raul chuckled. "Oh yeah! Did we forget to mention we go to Wolfglade?"

Derrick nodded with wide eyes. "Oh yeah. I would say you forgot to mention that."

The rat laughed and extended his arm to shake Derrick's paw. "I'm Paul. Sorry about my wolf friends . . . They are weirdos."

Lowe reached back and smacked Paul on the head. "Watch it, rat!" He chuckled.

Derrick smiled. "Well . . . I certainly have changed my opinion about Wolfglade. You guys are pretty cool."

Paul smiled. "Thanks man! Wolfglade is an awesome school. All the wolves are pretty cool folks; they are all pretty accepting of the minorities of everyone else there."

Derrick sighed. "Sound awesome . . . I wish I could go there. It sounds much better than Tigerthorn."

"I think it may be because of the name of the school. Tigers are lame. Wolves are cooler," Lowe joked.

Derrick laughed. "I hear you on that one. One of the bullies in our school is a tiger, and I really don't like him . . ."

Raul sneered. "Yeah . . . Tigers disgust me!" He turned down the road that led to Frankie's house. "You're a cool guy, Derrick. If you ever want to hang out with us, we can give you our numbers and hang with you when you need it."

Derrick handed Raul his phone. "Okay! Here you go. Just put your numbers in . . ." He watched as they all put their numbers in his phone.

Paul was the last one to put his number in. However, as he finished, he smirked. "You have Cassidy Wells' phone number? Hmm . . . Does someone have a crush?"

Derrick's fur stood up. "Yeah . . . We were friends before she left for Hollywood. She's been trying to rebuild all of her friendships that she left behind. But . . . yes, I have a crush on her."

Raul parked in Frankie's driveway, turned off the car, and turned around. "Well, have you told her?"

Derrick looked down. "Well . . . It is slightly complicated . . ." He told them a shortened version of what had happened in the theater with Cassidy.

They all gave him a wide-eyed stare. "Well . . ." Raul said. "That does sound complicated . . . Good luck with that, then."

Paul handed him back the phone and waved. "See you later."

Derrick got out of the car and waved back. "You can be sure of that!"

They waved at him and drove off.

Derrick walked into the living room of Frankie's house and sat down on the couch.

Frankie stood in the doorway and looked at him. "And just where have you been?"

Derrick sighed. "I hung out with Cassidy, went to see my mom, walked Cassidy home, and got driven home by some of the guys from Wolfglade." He smiled, "You know, those guys are actually pretty nice!"

Frankie's eyes widened. "Wow . . . You've had a packed day. Wait . . . WOLFGLADERS?!"

Derrick nodded. "Yeah. They aren't that bad."

Frankie freaked out. "BUT THEY ARE FROM AN OPPOSITE SCHOOL! They are also weird . . ." Someone knocked on the door, and Frankie went to open it. "I don't want my best friend's mind to be infected by those wolves." He threw the door open and gaped at the two wolves and rat on the other side of the door. "Uh . . . Hi . . ."

Raul smirked. "Hello cat." He looked past him at Derrick who had followed Frankie to the door. "Hey, Derrick. You left your wallet in the car. It fell out of your pocket."

Derrick smiled and took his wallet. "Thanks guys!" He narrowed his eyes. "Now give me back my keys and ID."

Raul and Lowe both turned to look at Paul who chuckled. "Dude! How'd you know that I did that?" He took the keys and the ID out of his pocket and handed them back. "Sorry man . . . Bad habits, I do that every time I meet new people." He chuckled nervously.

Derrick smirked. "I always have my keys in my back pocket, and they aren't there anymore, and I can usually tell when something is missing from my wallet."

Frankie awkwardly glanced at them, "Uh . . . How much of what I said did you hear?" He chuckled nervously.

Lowe shrugged. "Well . . . I don't know. We're just Wolfgladers trying to poison you best friend's mind." He and his friends laughed along, and Derrick joined in.

Frankie chuckled dryly. "Oh . . . So, all of it then. Oh, that's just brilliant!" That just made everyone else laugh a lot more. "OH, COME ON! That's not right."

Raul coughed. "Sorry . . ." He laughed. "Has anyone ever told you that you are an easy target for teasing?"

Frankie sighed. "I hear it 24/7 . . ." He walked into his room. "I'm going to bed . . ." He was followed by laughter, lots and lots of laughter.

Chapter 7

THE DAY OF THE DANCE HAD arrived, and Derrick had just finished school for the day and had to get ready for the dance. He walked into the theater and went to the backstage area, hoping to not run into Ernesto, but no such luck. Ernesto had chosen that day to check on the costumes.

"Ah! Derrick! Glad you came by today." He put a paw on Derrick's shoulder as he walked up. "I need you to work the night shift. I got a big production tomorrow, and everything in this theater needs to be clean in time for the show."

Derrick's eyes widened. "B-But Ernesto . . . I kind of had plans tonight. Really big plans . . ."

Ernesto nodded. "I know. You wanted to go to that dance tonight, but I need you here. I am sorry, kid, but life is not all about you. Besides, I'm not asking you, I'm telling you."

Derrick mumbled. "Oh, trust me . . . I know. You make it hard to forget."

Ernesto gave him a look. "Did you say something, kid?"

Derrick coughed. "Oh yeah! There's nothing I'd rather do with my night . . ." He said sarcastically.

Ernesto clapped him on the back. "That's the spirit, kid! I want you to be done by the time I get back at 12." He turned to walk away.

"Wait . . . Where are you going?" Derrick asked as he looked at Ernesto.

Ernesto turned. "Oh, you know, sponsoring that dance I just said you couldn't go to. Got to make sure my money is put to good use." He chuckled and handed Derrick his list. "Do these jobs, be done by twelve. And you better still be here when I get back." He pointed at him with a smile. "You'll get your normal paycheck." He chuckled and left the theater.

Derrick sighed and looked at the list. He had been given about thirty big jobs, and he had to do them all in ... He looked at his watch, which read 4:30. Seven and a half hours ... That may have seemed like a lot of time, but Derrick knew that he couldn't get all the jobs done alone in that time frame. He would have called Rowley and Frankie, but he didn't want to ruin the dance for them.

He looked at the list and read the first job. Clean the mirrors in both bathrooms. Derrick sighed; that was easy enough ... but he hated cleaning mirrors. He went to the janitor's lounge, changed into his uniform and got to work on the long list of jobs.

About two hours had passed since he had started on his jobs. He had finished about five of the jobs and had just started cleaning the concession stands. He had gotten several texts from his friends but had ignored them so they didn't try and ruin their night just to come help him out. He went into the back, got some soda to restock the soda fountain, and stacked the cups beside it.

He ducked under the counter to check everything, but when he came back up, someone was in front of the counter. He jumped and yelped. "CAIN!? How long have you been standing here?"

Cain glared at him. "It doesn't matter. I am here to get you to go to the dance." He motioned to Derrick's phone. "They have been trying to get ahold of you, and they are pretty upset you're avoiding them."

Derrick sighed. "I know I've been avoiding them, but I have to work so I can't go to the dance." He showed Cain his list of jobs. "I have to do all of these by 12 ... And I have finished five of them so far ... I wouldn't have been able to make it even if I tried, and to make it worse, if I am not here when Ernesto gets back, I will not only lose my job, but also my chance for college!"

Cain looked at the list, and his eyebrows went up as he read. "Clean the trash cans? Change the lightbulbs?" He looked up at Derrick. "Clean the gum off the bottoms of the theater seats? Derrick, this isn't a job; this is torture." He put a paw on Derrick's shoulder. "He's trying to keep you from the dance. He got paid off to keep you here." He showed him a video off his phone of Razor handing money to Ernesto and them whispering, but he could hear enough to know that Cain told the truth.

Derrick frowned. "Oh, well. Then I can't go." He turned and started cleaning out the popcorn machine.

Cain folded his arms. "Oh no, you don't. You made a promise, and you are going to keep it." He folded the list of jobs and put it in his pocket. "Because I am going to do all of your jobs for you, so you can get your tail to that dance."

Derrick shook his head and tried to get his list back. "I can't! I'll get into a lot of trouble."

Cain growled. "You. Are. Going."

Derrick cringed. "Um ... okay ... I just got to go talk to my superior."

Nathan came out of his office. "It is okay, I heard it all and completely agree with him. You are going to that dance."

Derrick's eyes widened, and he mumbled. "Nathan, you aren't supposed to do that ..."

Nathan rolled his eyes. "Do you really think I give a rip about what my father told you? I don't even like my dad." He shot Cain a look. "But I do like the fact that the guy taking your place is bigger and stronger than you."

Derrick gave Nathan a look. "HEY!"

Nathan smirked. "If you want to stay here and work, though ..."

Derrick's eyes widened; he really didn't want to stay here and work all night, and most certainly wanted to see Cassidy. "Okay. I'll go ... but I don't have a car."

Cain shrugged. "Get your costume. I'll get you a ride to the dance."

Derrick looked around as they walked down the alley behind the theater in his Phantom costume. "Why are we walking this way?"

Cain sighed. "I have a friend that lives back here that can take you to the dance, and Ernesto would never know." He walked up to an old van parked off to the side of the alley and banged his fist on one of the doors.

Derrick heard a voice on the inside yelling, "Oi! I am tryin' to sleep in 'ere!" The car door opened, and Derrick jumped when an overgrown lizard with an eyepatch over his left eye and dressed in rags aimed a gun at his face. "WHO ARE YOU, AND WHADYA WANT?!"

Cain stepped in front of Derrick and blocked him. "Relax, Gus. It's just me and a friend of mine."

Gus lowered the gun and hugged Cain. "CAIN! Good to see you. You have no idea how lonely I have been; we really need to hang out more!" He looked at Derrick and smiled. "Hi! My name is Augustus Silviano, but you can call me Gus." He stuck out his scaly hand.

Derrick smiled back. Yes, this guy did smell bad, and he literally lived out of a van in a dark alley, but he seemed like a nice guy. He shook the lizard's hand. "Nice to meet you, Gus. I'm Derrick."

Gus smiled and pulled Derrick into a hug. "IT IS NICE TO MEET ANOTHER PERSON!" Derrick hugged back and ignored the smell because this guy seemed like a really nice guy. It's not every day you get hugged by a guy you just met, after all. He pulled away and gave them a kind smile. "What can I do for you guys today?" He asked, leaning against his van.

Cain smiled a little. "I need a favor. This kid needs to get to a dance. He needs a ride to Tigerthorn."

Gus smirked. "That explains the costume." He motioned for Derrick to get in the van and turned to Cain. "I'll get him there and back. Any particular time he has to be back?"

Derrick poked his head out of the van. "I have to be back by before twelve, or Ernesto will have my head!"

Gus nodded. "Okay. Good. I can do that." He got into the driver seat and turned to look at Derrick. "Be careful with all of that stuff back there. It's kind of all that I have . . ." He put the keys into his ignition and turned on the car.

Derrick looked around the back of the van. "You have some really cool stuff back here, Gus! Where did you get it all?" He looked through a box of worn out baseball cards.

Gus smiled at Derrick through the rearview mirror. "I found a lot of that stuff at small garage sales, but a good portion of it people were throwing out, so I just took it." He frowned. "It's sad people that throw stuff out, when there are others that need it. Yesterday, I had bought two burgers and was going to eat them back at my van when I saw a raccoon, just a kid, I tell ya, digging through the trash. I invited him back to my van to share a burger with me." Gus sighed. "The kid is living in a box with only the clothes on his back, a blanket, and a Bible . . . I am thinking about inviting the kid to live here . . . But of course, I would need the law's permission . . ."

Derrick smiled and patted Gus's shoulder. "That is awfully nice of you, Gus. I am sure the kid would love it."

Gus sighed. "I sometimes think that being a soldier for 10 years of my life was a waste of time, seeing how I fought for our country, and when I come back, there are people like that poor kid with nothing, ya know."

Derrick sighed. "I hear you. My dad served in the military, and apparently not very many people know how to give respect to soldiers anymore . . ."

Gus looked up. "What did you say your name was?"

Derrick smiled. "Derrick. Derrick Hilman."

Gus looked in the mirror at Derrick. "Hmmm, where have I heard that name before?"

"I don't know. Maybe you served with him before he died."

Gus looked as if he was deep in thought as he turned into the school parking lot.

Derrick put his mask on as they pulled up to the school. "Thanks for the ride, Gus." He gave Gus his number. "Call me at 11:45."

Gus smiled and gave him a pat on the shoulder. "Go get 'em, kid!"

Derrick smiled and got out of the van and walked toward the school.

Cassidy stood by the side of the big gymnasium that had been turned into a party hall with a big dance floor in the middle of it. She had come dressed as her favorite fictional character, Red Riding Hood. She stood near the punch table looking for the strange dressed up Phantom, but also kept her eyes peeled for Derrick.

Elena stood near her and drank a cup of punch. "Maybe he isn't coming." She was dressed as a rock star. She scanned the crowd, her eyes stopping on a certain fire fighter. Her eyes lit up when she recognized him. "ROWLEY!" She scampered across the dance floor and tackle hugged him.

Cassidy chuckled as an embarrassed Rowley smiled at her. "I am glad to see you, too, El-Elena!"

Elena just stared down at him with a smile, "I'm not just glad to see you . . ." She got off of him and helped him up. "I am thrilled to see you, too." She leaned in close to him and kissed him.

Rowley squeaked, nervous and surprised, but he kissed her back.

Cassidy watched with a surprised look. Her best friend was kissing someone. Yeah, she had known about that crush for the longest time; but now Elena was kissing Rowley. She was grateful that her best friend had found someone . . . but she had always wanted . . .

"Hello, Little Red . . ."

Cassidy turned and saw the mysterious Phantom standing behind her. "You came! You actually came!"

The Phantom smiled. "Yes, my fair lady. I have come. I take care to keep my promises." He took her paw and kissed it. "It's a pleasure to see you again, Cassidy."

Cassidy smiled. "Okay, my dear sir." She said, mocking the Phantom's accent.

The Phantom chuckled and led her to the edge of the room to the refreshment table. "You're curious, aren't you?"

Cassidy shrugged. "Well, I am very interested in who you are. You're mysterious, kind, funny, and apparently you fancy me."

The Phantom smiled. "Oh really? How can you tell that?"

Cassidy chuckled and picked up a pineapple. "Because you are following the example of real gentlemen that you read about in those books. Gentlemen aren't usually gentle unless they are smitten for a girl . . . That's the kind of guy I am looking for."

The Phantom stood silent and still.

Cassidy gave him a look. "Would you take off that mask and show me who you are under there? I want to know who my gentleman is . . ."

The Phantom chuckled. "Wouldn't you like to know. I am not going to say."

Cassidy chuckled and walked around him. "Well . . . you aren't going to make this any easier for me, are you? What if I asked you questions to figure out who you are?"

The Phantom nodded. "Of course. Ask away."

Cassidy smiled and thought hard. "What is your opinion about Shakespeare?" She asked.

The Phantom relaxed. "I think he was a great writer and an amazing poet. The best writer that ever lived. A real credit to the world."

Cassidy smiled. "So you think highly of him?"

The Phantom smiled. "Who wouldn't? He is the best playwright in the world! I mean, his works are read in school, theaters, and even movies. The man has had an amazing impact on the world of literature."

At one point, the Phantom's accented voice cracked, and she thought she recognized the voice. "You sound oddly familiar; do I know who you are behind that mask. As in . . . in reality . . ."

The Phantom nodded. "Yes. You do know me. You've known me for a while."

Cassidy smiled. "Is that so?" She walked around him. "Are you a senior? Because if you're a junior or a freshman and you are flirting with me, I am going to kick your butt. But if you know me as well as you say you do, you already know how big a butt-whooping I can dish out."

The Phantom nodded and put his paws up in surrender. "Oh gosh . . . Please don't. I have seen what you can do . . . I am a senior"

Cassidy chuckled. "That's what I thought." She smiled and opened her mouth to ask another question, when Phantom of the Opera came over the speakers. She smirked and looked at the Phantom. "Someone heard you were coming, apparently . . ."

The part of the Phantom's face she could see blinked in surprise as he turned to look over at the sound booth.

Frankie chuckled as he played the Phantom of the Opera song. He watched as Derrick and Cassidy continued talking, with Cassidy thinking Derrick was some mystical Phantom. He had been slightly jealous from watching all the couples on the dance floor talking or chatting or, like Elena and Rowley, kissing. He had personally set them up because he could see how much they liked each other.

As soon as the Phantom of the Opera finished playing, he took the mic. "Hello people! This is DJ K-Dawg live at Tigerthorn, and we are gonna be laying down some sick beats tonight." He queued up another song.

Turner sat on one of the speakers, looking really bored.

Conner and Alex came and stood in front of him. Conner was dressed as US Soldier, and Alex dressed in a leather jacket and blue jeans. Conner gave Turner a weird look. "Has anyone ever told you that K-Dawg is not really a dog?"

Turner sighed and glared up at Frankie. "What?!" He said sarcastically. "I couldn't tell he wasn't a dog!" He put his head in his paws, "It's sometimes sickening . . . He doesn't even like canines."

Alex patted him on the back. "It's okay, Turner. Maybe he'll let you do stuff today . . ." He gave Turner the once over. "He didn't give you a costume!?"

Turner frowned. "Yeah . . . He said roadies don't need costumes." He slightly smiled. "Should I kick his tail later?"

Conner smirked. "Oh, for sure!"

Turner smiled and slid of the speaker to give them both a hug. "Thanks for coming to talk with me. You have no idea how boring Frankie can get . . ."

"I heard that!" Frankie gave Turner a pointed look.

"I know!" Turner snapped. He smiled at them. "So, I like your costumes. Who did you come as?"

Conner smiled, "I am a soldier of the US army. My dad served in the army for a while, so he helped me make my costume." He smirked and jerked his thumb at Alex. "He came dressed as his doctor."

Alex punched him in the shoulder. "I came dressed as THE Doctor, not a doctor! Sheesh! Doesn't anyone here watch TV?" He started coughing and wincing in pain.

Conner gave his friend a look and patted his back. "It's okay, buddy . . . Just another coughing fit . . ."

Alex looked up at his friend with a weak smile between coughs. "I'll be okay . . . I-I am gonna go to the bathroom . . ." He walked shakily toward the bathroom, coughing up a storm.

Turner watched him go. "I don't think he's as okay as he says he is . . ."

Conner shrugged. "It's fine . . . He did have Leukemia when he was younger, but it hasn't been much of a problem lately." He still looked worried about his friend. "I'm gonna go see if he is okay . . ." He walked towards the bathroom.

Derrick was getting nervous. Cassidy asking a lot of questions . . . Did she know? Was she just toying with him? Whether she did or not, he still enjoyed her company, and he could tell she had been enjoying his.

Cassidy laughed. "Okay . . . I got it! What do you think of football?"

Derrick grimaced. "What kind of a question is that?"

Cassidy chuckled. "I am trying to narrow it down. What? Do you not want me to find out who you are? Or would you rather tell me?" She winked.

Derrick's knees went weak, and he just stood there, but he kept his balance. "I don't necessarily like it . . . but there are times that I am motivated to enjoy it."

Cassidy chuckled. "You just let me exclude almost all of the guys at the school and all of the Wolfgladers."

Derrick sighed. "I am making this too easy for you . . ."

Cassidy chuckled. "Oh yes, you are . . . But I am having a lot of fun with this. But just to let you know . . . when I find out who you are, I am going to hit you for putting me through this." She winked at him.

Derrick blinked and sheepishly smiled. Okay . . . now he really, really liked her a lot. He was about to reveal himself and tell Cassidy how he felt about her . . . but he saw Ernesto at the punch table just looking around with a smile on his face. If he took the mask off . . . who knew what Ernesto would do to him?! He sighed, "I would love to tell you . . . But I can't tell you now . . ."

Derrick stood a few inches away from her. He wanted to kiss her, but he almost couldn't move from being so nervous . . . But she was right there . . . He just couldn't let an opportunity pass out of his reach. He put his arms around her. She looked at him with a smirk, as if she waited for him to do it. He leaned in and kissed her. He couldn't believe he had actually done it, and even more surprised that she kissed back. As soon as he began to enjoy it, though, a chilling thought ran through his mind. Cassidy thought she kissed the Phantom . . . she didn't know it was him. He wished so hard that he could tell her that she was kissing him. Then all he would have to worry about is if she would reject him . . . and Ernesto.

She broke it off and looked into his eyes. "What was that for, Mr. Phantom?"

Derrick couldn't move, "Well . . . I-I . . . I mean the real me . . . has liked you for the longest time and have never said anything about it . . ."

Cassidy smiled. "Well . . . That is very sweet. I just wish . . ." She reached up to his mask and began to pull it off.

Derrick didn't stop her. But as soon as her fingers touched the mask, his phone started ringing the Phantom of the Opera theme. Cassidy sighed and removed her fingers. "You are getting a call . . ."

Derrick frowned and took it out and looked at it. Caller I.D. said it was an unknown caller, but he knew it had to be Gus. He put the phone to his ear. "Gus?"

"Hey. It's 11:45, Derrick. You said you needed to go?"

Derrick sighed. "Oh . . . This is really bad timing." He looked at Cassidy, who had stepped back a little. "I'll be right there . . ." He hung up and turned to Cassidy. "I am sorry . . . I have to go . . ." He turned away.

Cassidy frowned as he turned. "Wait!"

The Phantom stopped and turned halfway.

Cassidy stepped a little closer. "When will I see you again?"

The Phantom smiled. "I will let you know." He looked nervously around. "I really have to go." He turned and left.

Cassidy frowned and looked at the ground . . . And realized the Phantom had dropped something, a set of keys . . . She picked them up and ran after the Phantom. "Wait!" She went through several sets of doors till she got outside.

But she didn't see him anywhere. She looked down at the keys and saw that there was a tag on it. A tag that said "Janitor Keys."

Her eyes widened as she realized who her Phantom was. All the pieces had fallen into place. Only one guy could've ... "Oh ..." She smiled as a plan to get her Phantom to meet on her terms built up in her head.

Derrick hopped in the van. "Oh gosh, that was way too close. Hurry, Gus. We need to get back!"

Gus smirked and put the van into drive. "Have fun, kid?"

Derrick took the mask off and sighed, sitting in the back of the truck. "That was the best night of my life ..."

Gus smiled and went a little faster. "So, I am guessing you got the girl."

Derrick sighed. "She wore cherry flavored lip gloss ... I can't believe that I actually kissed her!" He looked at Gus. "I wish I could've told her! I feel so dumb that I was scared of one jackal firing me and not paying for my college ..." He put his face in his paws.

Gus sighed. "Kid. I am no expert on love. But I think that when you love someone, you need to overcome boundaries to get them. That is how you can tell that someone's love is true. They should be willing to do anything for you, and it is the same thing the opposite way." He chuckled. "That's as deep as I can go with something like that."

Derrick smiled. "That sounds right ..." He looked out the window as they pulled into the road behind the theater. "But how do I tell her that I am the one who met her tonight? What if she doesn't really like me the same way?"

Gus parked and turned around to look at Derrick. "And what if she does? Sometimes, the best thing to do if you don't know how to tell someone something is to just tell them. And if she loves you, she will listen and understand." He shooed Derrick out of the van. "Now, get outta here, you! Before your boss finds you missing."

Derrick smiled and gave Gus a hug. "Thank you." He ran into the back of the theater and found Cain working on collecting the costumes.

Cain looked up. "Good. You are back. I did all of the other jobs except for this one." He handed Derrick the list. He pointed at his janitor uniform. "Change into that and give me your costume." Derrick went and changed into his uniform and gave Cain the costume. Cain shoved it to the bottom of the load he had been working on. "Hurry and take these to the dry cleaner." Cain went out the back door. "See you later, Derrick."

Derrick walked through the theater and out the front door to take the costumes to the dry cleaners. He dropped the clothes off and promised the dry cleaner employee that he would be back to get the costumes back the next day.

As he walked back to the theater, he saw Ernesto's car pull up in the theater parking lot. Ernesto got out of the car, slammed the door, and stomped toward Derrick. "HILMAN. I thought I told you to stay at the theater."

Derrick took out the list, praying that he could pull this off. "Yes, sir. But the list said to bring all the costumes to the dry cleaners." He pointed to the list. "It says right here, sir, and I did it as you instructed."

Ernesto looked at the list, then back up at Derrick. "Why yes, it does . . . It's at the bottom of the list. Did you really do all of the stuff on this list?"

Derrick nodded. "Yes, sir. I did." He kept his eyes on Ernesto as he examined his expression suspiciously.

Ernesto nodded. "Okay. Let's go see how you did, shall we?" He gestured for Derrick to follow him inside the theater. He checked every single job and saw they were all done. Derrick reminded himself that he really needed to thank Cain later for the help he gave him.

Ernesto was impressed with the way his theater looked. "Well, Derrick, I have to say . . . when I left this theater earlier, I didn't expect you to get done. Now I see how wrong I was." He handed Derrick his paycheck. "Here is your paycheck, Derrick. You did an alright job." He growled and pushed Derrick toward the door. "Now, get out of here. Get some sleep."

Derrick got shoved outside. He couldn't believe it. Ernesto actually had fallen for it. His escapade wouldn't reach his ears unless Nathan said something. His head was still spinning from kissing Cassidy. He couldn't think straight; his only thoughts were on Cassidy. He wanted to tell her. To be with her. He needed her; without her nearby, he felt like he was going crazy.

He was pulled out of his thoughts by a blasting horn. "Umm, Dude? Get in, you moron!"

He smiled as he got into Rowley's Prius, and they took him home with them begging to hear every word of what happened with Cassidy at the dance. "You guys will never believe it."

Rowley and Frankie stared at him with wide eyes after he finished recounting what had happened at the dance. "WHAAAAAAAAAAAAAAAT?!"

Derrick leaned back on the sofa in Rowley's living room with a knowing smile. "I told you guys you wouldn't believe it."

Rowley gaped. "I woulda noticed, mate, but I was kinda busy . . ."

Frankie guffawed. "Oh yeah! Busy. More like busy making out with Elena."

Rowley's ears flattened. "She took me by surprise! What was I supposed to do?" He slammed the pillow he was hugging into Frankie's face. "Shut up! At least I have someone."

Derrick hissed. "That was harsh bro." He patted Frankie on the back. "It's okay, buddy."

Frankie growled. "Thanks, Derrick . . ." He glared at Rowley. "I'll show you one day . . ."

Rowley frowned. "I'm sorry, mate . . . Didn't mean to snap. I am just a little shy about it, that's all . . ."

Derrick sighed. "It looks like we all have lady issues . . ."

Frankie chuckled dryly. "Hooray for being teenagers. We get more problems in life than on one of Ferguson's Trig tests, and the price for getting them wrong is even worse than failing!"

Derrick sighed. "Can't argue there, Frankie."

Rowley smiled. "Well, at least we don't have to worry about this stuff over Christmas break. Aaaand we are off of work till January 6th!"

Frankie beamed. "Freedom!" he sang. "We have to hang with each other."

Rowley nudged Frankie. "You guys need to come over to my house. Mom is going to make her Christmas dinner." He smiled. "She said to invite you guys and to tell you that she is makin' her famous Christmas roast for you two carnivores."

Derrick and Frankie traded glances. Rowley's mom made the best roast ever, and she didn't ever eat it. But she loved making it and watching the two other boys enjoy eating the roast. They always said it was one of their favorite parts of Christmas. Every time, though, Rowley couldn't resist throwing playful jabs at them. "YES. Tell her we will be here. And we will bring presents," Derrick said with a beam on his face.

Frankie nodded. "Of course, we will." He looked at his watch and then sat up. "OH GOSH! It's 2 o'clock." He stood up. "We need to go home! I need my beauty rest!"

Derrick shook his head. "I don't think beauty rest can help you look better man." He laughed.

Frankie pulled him up. "Come on wise guy, we need to go. Let's let the peaceful herbivore get some sleep."

Rowley stood and yawned. "Come on, you two. Before this peace lovin' herbivore turns to violence." He playfully swatted at the two. "Get outta here. I'll see you soon." He pushed them out of the front door. "BYE!" He shut the door behind him, a smirk growing on his face and a plan forming in his head. He took out his cell phone and dialed a certain number.

He waited for someone to pick up the phone. "Hello?" Elena's voice grumbled from the other end of the line. "Who the hell is this, and why are you calling at two in the morning?"

Rowley couldn't help but smile. "H-Hey, Elena . . . It's Rowley."

Elena chuckled. "Hey cutie! You miss me, or did you want another kiss?"

Rowley's face heated up. "Both . . . But that wasn't what I called about. I need to ask a favor."

"Ask away."

"Well . . . My family is havin' a Christmas Dinner, and our mutual friend is gonna be there. What do you say you and Cassidy come over? It'd be a fun chance for our two lovebirds to connect and converse."

"Are you sure you are just thinking about Cassidy and Derrick?" Elena purred, her voice making Rowley's face burn. "I bet you are making that really nervous face right now and look really cute," she added.

"Well... I don't know. Maybe we could... Umm..." Rowley stammered. Elena was toying with him, and he knew she knew it.

Elena laughed. "I'll make sure that I am there. I wouldn't miss it . . . For Cassidy's sake . . . and yours." Rowley couldn't see her, but he knew if he could, she would be winking at him. "Love you, Aussie." He heard her blow a kiss and hang up the phone.

He slid down the door. "Oh gosh . . . I am definitely in love . . ."

Chapter 8

DERRICK SIGHED AND FUMBLED with his tie. It was Christmas Day, and he was getting for the Christmas party at Rowley's house, and they insisted that they all dress nice. He loved hanging out with Rowley and his family. It reminded him of how much he enjoyed spending time with his own family. He frowned as he remembered flashes of memories of the last Christmas they had together.

Nine-year-old Derrick ran into the living room and yelled with glee. "PRESENTS!" He smiled wide and ran to examine his presents. He shook one of the boxes under the tree. It made a clinking sound as the contents of the box shook around. He looked up at his mom and dad, who were standing in the doorway. "Mommy? Daddy? Can I open them!? Please?" He pleaded, giving his parents the famous puppy eyes.

June chuckled. "I think we can do a few before breakfast." She sat next to him on the floor and gave him a hug. She looked up at Devon. "We can do that, right hun?"

Devon smiled and sat on the other side of Derrick and put a Santa hat on his son's head. "I think that would be an amazing idea kid . . ."

Derrick's eyes widened. "Really? YAY!" He picked up the box he messed with and ripped the wrapping paper. He gasped when he saw a box of Legos. "LEGOS!" He hugged his mom and dad. "I love them, thank you!" He grinned. "Can I play with them now?" He smiled.

Devon smiled. "You still have so many presents. And you still haven't opened the one from Daddy!" Devon handed him a small box wrapped in gold paper.

Derrick opened it with glee and stared at a box. The box was made of cherry wood. He brushed his paw over the top of the box. "It's smooth!" He exclaimed. He opened it and gasped. Inside the box was a silver watch. On the topside of the box, there were words inscribed. "No matter where I am, no matter what you have done; I will always love you." Derrick took out the watch and tried it on. It was so big his paw fit through it without touching the sides of the watch.

Devon smiled. "It's probably way too big now . . . but when you are older, you can wear it. And look." He pointed at the face of the watch. "It says the same thing as the inside of the box."

Derrick smiled. "Dad . . . It's awesome!" He rushed his dad and gave him a huge hug, which Devon returned with a big smile. "I love you so much, Dad."

Derrick cried as he looked at the box that he had kept on his bedside. He sat down on the bed and opened the box and looked at the watch. He picked it up and put the watch on. It was a perfect fit. "I love you so much, Dad." He put his face in his paws. "I wish you were here to see me . . ." He dried his eyes and closed the box.

Frankie leaned in. "Come on, Derrick. We have to go." He stopped when he saw Derrick crying. "Hey buddy . . . You okay?" He came and sat next to Derrick. "You wanna talk."

Derrick hugged his friend. "Shut up and let me cry."

Frankie patted his friend on the back. "I am here for you bud. Cry all you want. But we should get going soon . . . Rowley has a big surprise for you." He smiled at Derrick.

Derrick looked at his friend. "He does?" He let go. "Well . . ." He wiped his eyes. "I'll be out in a minute.

Frankie patted him on the shoulder and left. "I'll be in the car, and don't worry about the presents; I have them taken care of." He gave his friend a sympathetic smile and left the room.

Derrick looked up, thinking of his dad. "I love you, too, Dad." He got up and finished getting dressed and got into the car.

He looked at Frankie, who looked back at him. "Better?" he asked.

Derrick nodded. "Thank you . . ." He hugged him.

Frankie smiled and hugged back. "Merry Christmas, Derrick."

Derrick walked up to the front door of Rowley's house, carrying a bunch of wrapped boxes. He looked at the door, then at his paws. He had no idea how he was going to let them know they were there. He looked at the doorbell and leaned forward and pressed it with his nose. He heard the ding dong, and then Rowley's voice yell, "I GOT IT."

Derrick smiled as Rowley opened the door. "Derrick!" The kangaroo was dressed in a white shirt and black slacks with a black bowtie. He helped Derrick bring the stuff in and then gave him a hug. "Merry Christmas! I am so glad you could make it." He let go of Derrick and hugged Frankie who had just walked up. "Come on in, mates!" He yelled, "MOM, THEY ARE HERE!"

Derrick and Frankie heard the familiar, accented yell of their friend's mom. "Hey boys! I am in the kitchen!" They headed toward the kitchen to say hello.

Rowley, however, hung back and waited until he was sure they were gone. He smirked and jumped up toward the top of the door frame and hung up a mistletoe. "This is for your own good, Derrick." He chuckled.

Derrick and Frankie walked into Rowley's kitchen and saw his mom pulling the roast out of the oven. They stopped and stared at the roast. It was twice as big as the one that she had made last year. She turned and gave them a huge smile. "There are my boys! Get over here and give me a hug."

Derrick and Frankie beamed at her and gave her a big hug. "Hey, Mrs. . . ." Derrick started to say when he was interrupted by her.

"Oh no, Derrick. We've had this talk before. Call me Momma Clara, okay? None of this Mrs. Manchester talk." She wagged her finger at him.

Derrick smiled. "It's good to see you Momma Clara."

Frankie smiled. "The roast is even bigger this year! Why'd you make it so big?"

Momma Clara smiled and started cutting the roast. "Well, I had to make enough for our other visitors. I was thrilled when I heard Riley say he invited his girlfriend and her friend."

Derrick's eyes widened; Rowley hadn't said anything about inviting Elena and . . . His eyes widened even more as he heard the doorbell ring.

Momma Clara called for Rowley. "RILEY! Get the door!"

Rowley yelled from the living room, "I am busy right now! And don't call me Riley in front of my friends! Derrick, can you get the door?"

Derrick sensed something was up, but he went to the door anyway and opened it . . . to find Cassidy on the other side. "Cassidy?"

"Hey, Derrick!" She smiled.

"What are you doing here? I didn't know you were coming." Derrick smiled, "Not that I am complaining!"

Cassidy looked confused. "Rowley invited Elena and I . . . He said you knew I was coming."

They were interrupted by a cough and turned to see Rowley with a video camera in his paws and a mischievous smile on his face as he pointed up.

Cassidy and Derrick looked up to see the mistletoe on the door frame. "That wasn't there before . . ." Derrick shot a look at Rowley, who smirked.

Oh, that kangaroo was so going to get it later.

"Come on mates!" He motioned for them to get on with it. "Tradition says you have to kiss when you are under the mistletoe."

Derrick looked from Rowley to Cassidy, who tried to conceal her grin. "Well . . . who are we to break tradition?" Cassidy, said smiling at Derrick. "It won't be so bad Derrick."

Derrick looked into her eyes. "Okay." He pulled her close to him and leaned in to kiss her. He drew away after a few seconds.

Rowley and Frankie were clapping. "That was beautiful!" Frankie said, wiping a tear.

Rowley chuckled. "Can you do it again? I missed some of it."

Elena walked through the door, closed it, and took the camera away from him. "No. It's your turn." She kissed him.

Rowley squeaked a little in surprise, but kissed her back.

It had been a great night. There were presents for everyone, and everyone had their fill of Momma Clara's amazing food. Derrick enjoyed every moment of it, though most of the time most of his energy was used trying to not stare at Cassidy. As the last present was opened, the others congregated into the kitchen.

Derrick moved to follow them all out into the hallway, but stopped when a paw touched his arm. He turned to see Cassidy. "Cass?"

Cassidy looked at him with a look he couldn't describe. "Hey . . . Derrick, can we go onto the porch?"

Derrick's mind raced. She wanted to talk to him alone. Did she know? What was he supposed to do? "Uh . . . Sure . . ." He followed her onto the porch and sat on the swing.

She sat next to him. "I wanted to ask you some stuff . . . relationship stuff . . . as my oldest guy friend and all . . ."

Derrick sighed as his heart fell. "Uhhh . . . sure. What kind of advice do you need?"

Cassidy leaned on his shoulder. "Well, remember that guy I told you about . . ."

Derrick chuckled as his heart shattered into a million pieces. "Yeah! Is the lucky guy anyone I know?"

Cassidy chuckled. "Yes. Most definitely. I just want his attention . . ."

Derrick sighed and put on a fake smile. "Hmm . . . and you want some ideas on how to get it?"

Cassidy smiled. "I would definitely love some . . ."

Derrick sighed. Even though he had just had his heart shattered, he would not refuse her get ahold of the guy that made her happy. "Well . . . if the guy were me. I would want it to be spontaneous and something that I would never be able to miss, even if I tried."

Cassidy gave a sly, little smile. "Hmm . . . Wow. That was some amazing advice."

Derrick smiled. "Anything for my . . ." He swallows. "oldest girlfriend . . ." He faked a convincing smile.

Cassidy smiled. "Thank you so much!"

Frankie peeked out. "Hey Derr . . ." He saw them. "Oh . . . Umm . . . was I interrupting something?"

Derrick sighed. "Oh . . . no. She was just asking for advice . . . about a guy . . ."

Frankie's eyes widened a little. "Oh . . . Well we have to go . . . Come on, Derrick. Rowley is staying the night at our house . . ." He left without another word.

Cassidy got up awkwardly. "Umm . . . I am sorry if I am keeping you."

Derrick got up. "I am sorry, Cass . . . It's not your fault." He smiled shakily. "I hope you get your guy." He turned and walked out of the porch, said his goodbyes, and went to the truck in a rush.

Rowley followed. "Derrick?!" He opened the back door of Frankie's truck and saw Derrick lying in a miserable heap. His expression softened as he climbed in the truck and sat next to him. "'Ey mate . . . What's the matter?"

Derrick lifted his head and sniffled. "C-Cassidy likes another guy . . ." He put his head back down and started crying again. "To her, I am just her oldest guy friend."

Rowley sighed. "Oh, Derrick . . . I am so sorry, mate . . . I had no idea." He sighed, "I wish I knew what to say to you right now . . ." He gave Derrick a look. "How about a hug, mate?"

Derrick looked up at Rowley for a while and then sat up and hugged Rowley super tight. "I just can't . . ."

Rowley sighed and hugged back. "Don't'cha be worrying yourself over this, okay?"

Frankie opened the door by the driver's seat and peaked in. "Derrick?"

Rowley shushed him. "He's right here . . . Just get in the car and drive." He patted Derrick's back and let the wolf hug him.

Frankie nodded somberly, got into the truck, put the keys into the ignition, and drove them home.

Chapter 9

IT WAS JANUARY 6TH, TWO WEEKS after the Christmas party, and school was beginning again. But Derrick wasn't awake. He still slept. He hadn't really done much since he had gotten home that night; he mainly just sulked around the house, ate, slept, showered, and did an awful lot of moping.

Frankie sighed as he watched his friend sleep. Derrick had looked so hurt and dejected those last two weeks, and Frankie missed seeing that spark of fun and joy in Derrick (even if it had only been gone for two weeks). He honestly felt super bad for the timber wolf. So, he did the first thing that he thought of. He took all of his pop tarts from all of his secret hiding places and dumped them onto Derrick's bed.

Derrick woke up with a jolt as he got covered in tinfoil-wrapped toaster pastries. "Frankie? What the hell . . . ?!" He looked a little bit ticked off and really annoyed. "Why are there pop tarts all over me?"

Frankie sat down next to him on the bed. "It's all of them . . . All of the pop tarts from every single one of my secret hiding places."

Derrick's eyes widened. "All of them? What?! Why?"

Frankie sighed. "I have watched my best friend in the entire universe mope around for the last two weeks . . . and I have honestly felt just as bad as you do. So, I am giving you all of my pop tarts so I can have at least a slight chance to have my best friend back."

Derrick stared at Frankie and the pop tarts and sniffled. "You're doing this for me?" He teared up a little.

Frankie gave his friend a hug and tried to comfort him the best he could. "You good now?"

Derrick nodded and looked up. "Y-Yeah . . . I think I am ready for school . . ." He got out of his bed and went into the bathroom to shower and change into some fresh clean clothes.

Frankie went into the kitchen and just messed around on his phone. Suddenly, his phone chirped. He looked at it and saw that it was a text from Rowley with a picture attached. He quickly read the text with wide eyes and clicked on the picture to make sure it was what he thought it was and ran back into the bedroom and yelled, "Derrick! You need to get to school. Rowley just saw something you would not believe."

Derrick popped his head out of the bathroom, his body wrapped in a towel and his fur dripping. "What?!"

Frankie turned away. "GET BACK IN THERE AND FINISH SHOWERING! You'll find out when we get to school."

Derrick rolled his eyes and shut the door. "I was wrapped in a towel, you know." He yelled.

Frankie crossed his arms and chuckled. "I just didn't want you getting my carpet wet."

Derrick laughed. "Ha! Such a sissy."

Frankie sighed. "Good to have you back, Derrick." He said through the door. He heard Derrick mumble to himself and then start quoting Phantom of the Opera and rolled his eyes. He walked back into the kitchen. "And here I was, getting used to the lack of the Phantom of the Opera in this house."

Derrick looked super antsy as Frankie pulled into the school parking lot. "Come on, Frankie! Park!" He looked at the school, trying to see if he could see what Rowley wanted him to see.

Frankie stopped before going to park and glared at his parking space. "I would . . . BUT THERE'S A FREAKING KANGAROO IN IT!"

Derrick looked out the front windshield and saw Rowley standing in the parking space with a look on his face and a piece of paper in his paw. Frankie beeped his horn at Rowley, and he begrudgingly stepped out of the parking space.

Derrick got out of the car. "Hi!" He walked up to Rowley and hugged him. "Whad'ya want me to see?"

Rowley smiled a little. "This should make you feel a little better." He handed Derrick the paper. "Cassidy's been puttin' these up around the school. ALL OVER. Kids are walkin' around with these plastered on their backs."

Derrick read the paper, and his eyes widened, then read it aloud. "Dear Mystery Phantom, I would really like to meet up with you today after school. If you like me as much as you say you do, please meet me at the place you first met me as the Phantom at 3:15. From Cassidy Wells . . ." He looked up at his friends. "She took my advice . . . Oh my gosh . . ."

Rowley sighed. "You are going tonight. You have to end this charade. It cannot go on any longer."

Derrick nodded. "I have to . . . And . . . When I do . . . I am going to tell her how I, as in me, Derrick Hilman, feel about her."

Frankie smiled. "There you go man. That's how you do it."

Derrick smiled. "Now, if you don't mind. I am gonna go help Cassidy pass these out."

He walked into the school and weaved his way through the hallways, trying to find Cassidy.

When he finally found her, he found she was being pestered by Razor, who waved one of the signs in her face. "What the heck is this, Cassidy? You chasing after some imaginary person who doesn't even really exist?"

Cassidy shrugged. "Maybe . . . Oh! Are you still jealous he's gotten a kiss from me and you haven't?" She got in his face.

Razor stared menacingly at her for a second, then turned to walk away. He slammed the sign into Derrick's chest as he passed. "Looks like neither of us are getting the girl, Hilman." He kept walking.

Derrick winced but smiled. *"Is that so?"* he thought. *"Because I am sure that I have an invitation to answer."* He chuckled and walked up to Cassidy. "Morning, Cass!"

Cassidy turned. "Derrick!" She gave him a hug. "I am so glad to see you are feeling better. Frankie said you were a little under the weather."

Derrick's smile faltered for a split second, but he didn't think she had noticed. "Oh, did he?" He is so gonna kill him later. "Yeah, I am." Which wasn't technically a lie . . . He wasn't moping in his room anymore, and he had just found out he may actually have a chance with the girl of his dreams. He definitely felt a lot better than he had before

Cassidy smiled. "That's good! Do you like the posters? I decided to take your advice and post them all over the school. Do you think my guy will notice it?" She looked around, worried.

Derrick smiled and gave her a side hug. "Don't worry; he'd have to be blind not see this. Plus, I am pretty sure he has already seen it."

Cassidy smiled, still looking around. "Yeah . . . I bet he has."

Derrick looked around at all the posters. "So Principal Lester let you put all of the posters up?"

Cassidy's face drained of color. "We're supposed to ask before we put posters up?"

"MISS WELLS!" an angry voice broke through the crowd of students as Principal Lester, a huge barn owl, made his way towards them. He showed them one of her posters. "Miss Wells . . . is this your idea of a joke?"

Derrick spoke up. "Umm . . . sir . . . this was my idea. She is just trying to get a guy's attention, and as her best friend, I wanted to help her."

Cassidy gave him a side glance. "Derrick, you don't have to get in trouble for this. I did it by myself, Principal Lester."

Derrick looked at Cassidy. "I gave you the idea, so I am a fellow conspirator."

Principal Lester gave them both a look. "Both of you. My office, now."

Cassidy gave Derrick a look as they followed the principal. "What the heck was that for!? I came up with the idea to hang the posters up around the school. You should not be coming to the office with me."

Derrick gave her a side-glance. "I am sorry, Cass, but as your oldest guy friend and best friend, I am your . . ." he gave her a slight smirk. "co-conspirator . . . Just like old times." He winked at her.

Cassidy couldn't help but smile at Derrick. "Yeah . . ." she giggled. "What do you think our punishment will be?

"I am very disappointed in you both, and since you both were part in creating and hanging up these posters, you both have to pick up every single one of them." Principal Lester crossed his wings. "You are lucky . . . I could've gone a lot harder on you two . . . but you have only been here for a few months, Miss Wells, and Mr. Hilman obviously didn't know about it till he arrived this morning; so, I am letting you off easy." He smiled a small smile and handed them each a trash bag. "Now, get outta here you two."

Derrick and Cassidy nodded and took their trash bags. "Thank you, sir," Cassidy said as she walked out the door behind Derrick.

The principal smiled. "You two have fun, now!" He chuckled as he went back to his work.

As they walked out of the main office and out into the hallway, Cassidy turned and slugged him on the shoulder. "You and your best friend speech! I could've taken the punishment alone." Her ears flattened, and she calmed down. "Thank you . . ."

Derrick winced. "Make up your mind, Cass! Are you mad or glad?"

She smirked. "A little bit of both!" She smiled. "Come on . . . Let's get these posters gathered up." She threw a playful punch at him.

Derrick smiled at her. "Okay." He chuckled as she punched him.

They spent until lunch going through the hallways and taking down posters and laughing at old memories they brought up. All through the rest of the day, Derrick became more and more confident about coming clean to Cassidy about everything. He even left school early so he could get there early.

Cassidy stood on the stage alone, waiting for her Phantom to show up. She wondered if maybe the posters on the wall were a little bit too much. Maybe he had gotten nervous and decided not to show his face out of nerves.

"Cassidy."

She whirled around to see the Phantom standing behind her. She smiled and hugged him. "You came! I almost thought that you weren't coming."

The Phantom chuckled. "It's hard to miss. There were signs all over the school. I noticed very quickly. I watched you and your friends hang them up."

Cassidy smiled. "I had a friend give me the idea . . . I wanted to talk to you . . . Set some things straight."

The Phantom stayed still as she spoke, watching and listening for her to continue.

She walked a step closer. "Being with you at that dance . . . I can't lie, it was amazing. You are amazing . . . But I don't like you."

The Phantom looked surprised. "You don't?"

Cassidy shook her head and took another step forward. "The guy I like is . . . funny and cute, and he knows me better than any other guy I know . . ." She gave the Phantom a sharp look. "And if he doesn't take off that mask right now, I am going to knock him to the moon."

Derrick's eyes widened. She knew . . . Oh my gosh, she knew. He slowly reached up and took the mask off. "You got me . . ." His ears flattened, and he chuckled. "I had no idea that you felt that way, Cass . . ."

She put a paw on his face. "Is there something you want to tell me, Derrick, before I slap you for putting me through all of this?"

He nodded. He stared into her eyes. "Cassidy Wells . . . I love you. I have loved you for as long as I have known you, and I cannot tell you how much I have tried to tell you, but I could never do it . . . But here and now, I am going to say it. I love you." He winced, waiting for her to slap him.

She reeled her arm back as if she was going to slap him, but instead of slapping him, she grabbed him by the collar of his costume, pulled him towards her, and kissed him.

Derrick blinked in surprise, but the surprise was short-lived, and he wrapped his arms around her and began to kiss her back. This went on for a few minutes before he pulled away and blinked again. "Whoa . . ."

She smirked. "I'll take that as a compliment." She punched him in the arm.

"OW!" He winced and rubbed his arm. "What was that for?!"

She glared. "For what you put me through, Mr. Phantom!" She slowly smiled. "But it was romantic."

He chuckled. "How'd you figure it out?"

She took a set of keys out of her pocket and dangled them in front of his face. "These look familiar?"

"Why I wore that with my costume, I have no idea." He giggled and hugged her. "Hey . . . This is fun and all, but I have got to punch in soon, and if Ernesto saw you with me, he'd blow a gasket . . . Maybe we could meet for dinner soon? A real date?"

She kissed him on the cheek. "It's a date, Derrick." She smiled and turned to walk away. "See you around."

Derrick stared at her with a goofy grin as she walked away, but he quickly snapped out of it and went to get changed for work.

In the shadows by the sides of the theater, someone pressed the stop recording button on their phone as Cassidy walked away. "Just wait till my dad sees this." Lorena chuckled as she walked out of the theater, careful to avoid Derrick.

Chapter 10

DERRICK HAD QUICKLY JOINED his friends, and in a good two and a half hours, they had finished their jobs. Derrick had told them how it had gone, and they were thrilled!

"Oh my gosh mate! I am so proud of you!" Rowley hugged him tight.

"That's my best friend!" Frankie put Derrick in a headlock and gave him a noogie.

Derrick giggled. "Guys, come on! Give me some room to breathe . . . I'm still thinking this was a dream . . ."

Rowley looked past him and frowned. "Well, it looks like that dream is about to become a nightmare . . ."

Derrick turned to see Ernesto walking towards them with a dejected-looking Nathan following, and he didn't look happy. He pointed at Rowley and Frankie. "You two, outside. Now. Go home or something. I need to talk to Derrick."

They both gave Derrick a look as they walked out the door. Derrick swallowed and looked at Ernesto. "What is it, sir?" He tried to look as respectful as possible.

Ernesto noted that. "Derrick, I am not happy with you right now. You didn't take my advice to stay away from the girl . . . but what upsets me more is that you disobeyed a direct order and went to that dance disguised as The Phantom." Derrick opened his mouth in shock, but before he could say anything, Ernesto added, "Lorena saw the whole thing and recorded it; now, do you want to lie and say it isn't true, because that would be useless right now!"

Derrick just shook his head, defeated. He looked at Nathan who had his head high in almost a defiant look.

Ernesto continued, "Now, I am not going to tear up your storybook ending, because I am not as big a monster as your perceive me to be . . . but I am going to have to give consequences for your actions."

Derrick nodded. "I accept them . . . I shouldn't have disobeyed you, sir . . ." He said this in all genuineness.

Ernesto nodded. "Good. Because you and Nathan will be cleaning the attic at my house tomorrow, so you can tell your friends they are off. Nathan will pick you up tomorrow and bring you to our house." He gave Derrick the once over. "You can go."

Derrick nodded and walked past them and went outside to the others.

"What happened, mate?" Rowley asked, concerned.

"He found out about me sneaking to the dance . . . and I am going to be cleaning his attic tomorrow as a punishment." Derrick shrugged, "It seems fair. He gave me an order, I disobeyed . . . at least he isn't firing me."

Frankie nodded. "Yeah. At least you still have a job."

Rowley sighed. "I don't like it . . . What if it's not what it seems?"

Derrick shrugged. "I am just going to be cleaning his attic. He's taking advantage of his step son." He turned. "Come on . . . Let's go . . . I need to rest . . ." He smiled and drifted off into a daydream about Cassidy.

Derrick walked through the halls of the school the next day with purpose. He avoided even acknowledging Lorena's existence, and he didn't have trouble with Razor and crew. When he walked by, Razor shouted at his friends, and his friends had their arms crossed and were not happy.

"No man. We are not doing that. It's wrong." Manny shook his head. "I am not getting arrested just because of your personal vendetta."

"Since when do you guys think!? It's just one guy I want to put in the hospital! What is the problem with that? You did it before!"

Buck glared. "Listen . . . If you have something to settle, do it now. He's right there." He pointed at Derrick, and Razor turned and glared. Buck turned Razor back to facing him. "But as long as you hold that attitude, we aren't supporting you." He and Manny turned and walked away.

Razor stomped after them. "Don't you dare walk away from me! I will ruin you morons!" His voice cracked and almost sounded pleading.

Derrick watched with wide eyes. Buck and Manny had just dissed Razor . . . He couldn't believe it . . . Those two actually had thought for themselves and decided to stop. He just shook his head and did a double take, then went to class with wide eyes.

At lunch, Cassidy and Derrick decided to merge the tables and sit together. He sat next to her, and she grabbed ahold of his paw. Conner and Alex chuckled and awwed at the new couple.

"I knew that he liked her, I just knew it!" Conner chuckled and looked at Alex. "I totally called it. Cough up my five bucks bro."

Alex sighed and pulled out his money. When both Cassidy and Derrick gave him a questioning look, he answered "He made a bet that Derrick liked you, and I bet against him."

Conner giggled. "And you loooooooooost! I was right! Yeah!"

Alex growled at Conner, which made the young wolf yelp and hide behind Cain.

Elena glared at Alex. "Down boy."

Alex turned back to his food. "Yes, Elena." He smiled at Conner, who shrunk back.

Elena smirked and patted Alex on the head. "Good boy." She chuckled.

Conner looked hurt. "But I am a good boy!"

Cain wordlessly put his paw on the younger wolf's head and gave it a few good scratches.

Derrick chuckled and turned to Rowley. "Looks like our group got bigger." He chuckled.

Rowley winked. "Like I always say, mate. No worries!" They both laughed.

Cassidy smiled. "It actually feels good to sit with everyone. Why didn't we think of this earlier!?"

Everyone at the table stopped eating and looked at each other.

"I don't know." Alex said thoughtfully.

Elena scratched her head. "We literally could have just invited these two to sit with us when we were planning to sit with you."

Cain grunted. "We coulda saved so much space."

Everyone stayed quiet, then after a while, they all started laughing.

Derrick heard a nervous cough and looked up. Buck and Manny were standing at the head of the table with their trays. "Uh . . . Derrick?" Buck asked. "You mind if we sit with you?"

Derrick cocked his head. "Uh . . . Sure . . . But what happened with Razor?"

Manny uncomfortably took the seat next to Cain. "He tried to get us to do something we didn't feel comfortable doing . . . so we told him no. He wasn't happy about that and started cursing at us in the middle of the hallway. He is in detention."

Cassidy smiled, "Well . . . you can sit here for the rest of the year if you like. Maybe Razor will come around."

Buck sighed, "I hope so . . . He's not really a very mean guy . . . He just doesn't like Derrick very much. He's actually really nice when it comes to us and the football team. The only bad thing he does is the fact that he makes us steal lunch money . . ." He looks sheepishly at Conner and Alex. "He never said that freshmen kicks hurt so much, though . . ."

Manny nodded. "Yeah . . . We're his only friends." He looked down at his plate.

Elena sighed. "Dang . . . Never thought I'd feel sorry for Razor . . ."

Frankie nodded. "You can say that again."

Derrick sighed. "I just wish I knew why he hated me . . ."

Buck shrugged. "That's something to ask him . . ."

Derrick nodded thoughtfully, contemplating in his head and wondering what he could've done to make Razor hate him so much.

Chapter 11

AFTER SCHOOL, NATHAN PULLED up in his truck to pick Derrick up. He got in the truck and buckled up as Nathan drove off toward his house. Derrick looked at Nathan. Nathan's had a grim expression, but other than that didn't reflect any other emotion. "I am sorry if I got you in trouble, Nathan."

Nathan sighed and shook his head. "It's not your fault, Derrick. What I did, I chose to do by my own choice. I wanted you to go to that dance; my dad just wanted money from it. Keeping you away got him fifty dollars; when he found out you went, he wasn't happy. But of course, he still has fifty dollars, so he isn't complaining yet."

Derrick sighed. "I guess I am just mad your dad doesn't even begin to compare with mine ... I just don't like him for taking my dad's place ... and I wasn't looking forward to siblings ..." He shot a look at Nathan. "No offense to you."

Nathan chuckled. "None taken bro." He smiled as he pulled into the driveway.

Derrick sighed. "I am sorry for being such a jerk to you ..."

Nathan gave him a look. "If anyone should be apologizing, it should be me. I wasn't a very good step-brother." He got out of the car. "I just wish I could do something to help you."

Derrick got out and followed him into his house. "You don't have to do that ... But I am sure you will think of a way anyway."

Nathan chuckled, and they headed to the attic.

They went up to the attic, avoiding Lorena's mocking stares and laughs. Ernesto waited for them in the attic next to a big stack of boxes. He looked up at Derrick and Nathan. "About time you two showed up."

Derrick sighed and looked around. The attic actually wasn't as messy as he thought it would be. There were just a few piles and boxes around. He looked at Ernesto. "So, what would you like us to do here, sir?"

Ernesto looked around. "Well . . . This place does need to be swept, and these boxes can be moved against the wall." He put his paw on his chin. "That is really all that needs to be done. After you're done, you can go."

Derrick looked relieved. "Thank you, sir. I'll try to get done by 5:30, so I'll be out of the way of your family."

Ernesto nodded, "Yes . . . the sooner the better if you don't mind."

Nathan coughed, "Okay . . . Let's get to work, Derrick . . ." He gave his dad a look. "We'll get your attic clean."

Ernesto nodded with an edge. "Thank you, Nathaniel." He turned and walked out of the attic.

Nathan glared after his dad. "What is he up to?"

Derrick shrugged. "I dunno . . . Maybe he is just on edge about something" He went over to a stack and picked up the one of the boxes on the floor next to it and carried it to the wall. "I am just glad my punishment isn't any worse."

Nathan shook his head and picked up the box next to the one Derrick had just picked up and went to put it next to his. "I don't know . . . He's being lenient . . . That's not like him . . ."

Derrick came to get the box on top of the stack. "Well . . . I still have a job, so . . ." As he turned to walk back to the wall, he tripped and fell, causing the contents of the box to spill on the floor. "OW!" He yelped as pain ran up his leg as his knee hit the floor.

Nathan dropped the box he carried and rushed to Derrick's side. "Are you okay, Derrick?"

Derrick nodded and sat up, rubbing his knee. "Yes . . . I just need a few minutes."

Nathan nodded and went to pick the papers that fell out of the box. He went to put them back into the box when he noticed something and froze. "Derrick . . . ?"

Derrick looked up from rubbing his knee. "What's up?"

Nathan looked down at the papers in his paws. "What was your dad's name?"

Derrick stood up but winced. "Oww . . . His name was Devon . . . Devon Hilman."

Nathan looked up at him with an angry look. "There are a bunch of letters from him to you and your mom here . . . From the looks of it . . . he's still alive."

Derrick rushed to his side in seconds, his knee not hurting as much. "WHAT?!" He took the letters from them. He read through one.

"Hey kiddo . . . This is your dad . . . I haven't gotten any response to any of my previous letters . . . I just hope you are actually getting these. By this time, my god-forsaken tour has kept me from 7 birthdays, 4 Christmas's, and probably countless more field trips and plays. I am sorry I have been gone for so long. After that attack on camp and my best friend going turncoat . . . I just can't get you or your mom outta my head. Sometimes, I wish I could be there with you . . . See you grow into the young wolf you are becoming. I love you son . . . If you are getting any of these . . . Please send me a letter . . . and a picture of yourself . . . I miss seeing your face, Son.

Sincerely, Devon Hilman, your dad.

A tear fell from his eye and down his cheek as he read. He scanned the other letters and found that there were several more like this. Derrick went from sad to angry when he saw that most of them were recent. He turned to Nathan. "He planted these here. He knew I'd find them. HE'S BEEN LYING TO US. THAT SICK . . ."

"Language, Derrick . . ." Nathan put a paw on Derrick's shoulder. "You're right, though . . . This is a sick way of showing he hates you . . ." He tried to get Derrick to calm down.

Derrick didn't want to calm down. He turned to leave the attic. He was going to face his demon, who he found in the living room reading a book non-chalantly. Derrick slammed the letters down on the table in front of Ernesto. "You lied to us. You told us he died, and then you married my mother . . . YOU SICK MONSTER!"

Ernesto blinked tiredly at the letters> "Oh . . . You weren't supposed to find those."

"OH, SHUT UP. You knew I would to find them. You probably even put them in that box! Right at the top of an open box." He growled. "Is this your idea of a punishment? Or do you just hate me? Maybe because I remind you too much of my dad, who you abandoned."

Ernesto shrugged. "Yeah, you have it all right. I do hate you. and your father. He married the perfect girl . . . Your mom. Devon was the perfect guy . . . And I got stuck on the sidelines of a relationship with a girl that I wanted myself. So yeah. I left your dad in another country and got his tour extended twenty years. And yes, I married your mom after telling everyone he was dead." He looked as if he was just relaying the weather to his kids.

Derrick growled, "And you do not see anything wrong with that?! You're crazy!" He turned. "Forget your stupid attic. I am going to tell my mother about this." He turned and walked out of the house.

Ernesto sighed and picked up the notes. He turned to Nathan, who stood in the doorway. "Can you put these somewhere, son?"

Nathan took the letters but glared at Ernesto. "You're not my dad . . . You're just a sick liar."

Ernesto sighed. "You can have whatever opinion about me you want, Nathaniel. But at least. can you just do something with these."

Nathan growled and walked off as his dad walked out the door with his phone to his ear. He made sure his dad had left. then went to his room and got out a pen, some paper, and an envelope.

Derrick walked into the hospital a half hour later. He walked to the front counter and asked to be admitted to see his mom. The raccoon at the front desk bit her lip. "I am sorry. Mr. Hilman . . . We have orders to not let you through."

Derrick glared, "May I ask who gave you the orders?"

The raccoon looked nervous. "Umm . . . Ernesto Claw . . ."

Derrick sighed. "I figured . . . That's why I am ignoring that order." He walked past the desk and into the hospital. He could hear the raccoon behind him flustered and trying to get him to come back. But he had his mind and heart set on going to see his mom. He had to tell her what Ernesto had done to them.

He had approached his mom's room when he saw Ernesto coming out her room followed by his mom's bed. He glared at Ernesto. "Mom!"

His mom saw him. "Derrick!" She smiled. "Ernesto said you were at work."

Ernesto fidgeted. "Who let him back here? Someone restrain him."

Derrick shook his head. "Mom, he lied to you. He's been lying to us . . . to you for years."

His mom gave him a look. "Derrick, I know you aren't fond of Ernesto, but you really should not accuse him like that."

Derrick pleaded with his mom. "But . . . He did, Mom! He's been lying and hiding the evidence. I saw . . ."

He got interrupted when Chet the Dragon came up behind him and grabbed his arm. "Mr. Hilman . . . I am going to have to ask you to leave."

Derrick growled. "Get your claws off of me." He jerked his arm away and glared at Ernesto. "You ruined my life, lied to me for six years, and you think your money will fix it, huh? Well, someone is going to expose you, and you are going to get what you deserve."

Ernesto glared at him, then looked at Chet. "Get him out of here."

Chet gave Derrick an apologetic look, then led him out.

Derrick broke away and glared at Chet. "Forgive me for being rude. but I can walk. I'll see myself out and away from you suckers." He started walking away.

Ernesto glared after him. "Hilman!" He shouted. "You're fired!"

Derrick just kept walking. Chet followed him. "Derrick . . . I am sorry about that. but . . ."

Derrick kept walking. "Oh no . . . I totally understand. What did he do to you? Pay you or threaten you?"

Chet frowned. "He said he'd cut his funding for the hospital if we didn't make an effort to keep you out . . ." He hung his head. "I'm sorry . . ."

Derrick sighed and stopped. He turned to look back at Chet. "I know . . . Please . . . Just take care of my mom . . ." He gave Chet a hug, then walked away. He went outside the hospital and sat down on the sidewalk and just started crying.

He cried for a while till his phone buzzed in his pocket. He took his phone out of his pocket and saw a number he didn't recognize. He wiped his eyes and answered. "Hello? This is Derrick . . ."

"Derrick? It's Raul." The voice on the other end said.

Derrick sat up and sniffled, trying to compose himself. "Oh. Hi! H-How'd you get my number?"

Raul sighed. "You gave your phone to us to put our numbers in . . . Remember? Am I calling at a bad time? Do you wanna talk?"

Derrick smiled. "That would be awesome."

"Sweet man. Well, there is a 'dog's night out' thing at your local Burger Binge. Apparently, food is fifty percent off, and soft drinks are free. That's where our football team will be hanging out tonight . . . But if you want some listening ears, you could use the time to vent instead? You need a ride?"

Derrick was grateful for the offer, but he couldn't help but ask. "Would you be able to take a plus one? I managed to tell Cassidy how I feel . . . and right now, I would really like to have her with me."

Raul chuckled. "Sure man. She can sit in the back with you and Paul. Just be careful. He is probably going to mess with you two." Derrick heard someone laughing in the background, and Derrick heard Raul sigh. "Actually, he guarantees he will."

Derrick chuckled. "Yes. Count us in." He quickly texted Cassidy, telling her about it. "Okay. Can you pick me up from the hospital?" He asked.

"Yeah man. I'll see you in about five minutes bro." Raul hung up.

Derrick smiled as Cassidy texted back, "Sure Derrick."

He texted back, "We'll be by in 15."

Chapter 12

DERRICK GOT IN THE BACK OF Raul's car and high fived Lowe and Paul. "Hey guys . . . Thanks for coming to get me."

Paul smiled. "Hey, Derrick!" He smirked a little. "Where's Cassidy?"

Derrick frowned more. "She's at her house . . ."

Raul gave Paul a look in the rearview mirror. "We're going to pick her up."

Lowe turned and also gave Paul a look. "Keep the flirting to a minimum. She does have a boyfriend now, and any of us can deck you at any minute."

Paul smirked and laughed with them, then his face turned all serious, and he pulled out a switchblade. "Try me wolf boi." He glared at Lowe.

Derrick sighed and gently grabbed Paul's arm. "Put the switchblade away, Paul."

Paul sighed and reluctantly put it away. "Fiiiiiiiiiine."

Raul looked at Derrick through the rearview mirror. "I am sorry man, I forgot to ask where I am going. Where does she live?"

"Umm . . . 324 Northside." Derrick chuckled. "I used to go all the time before she moved . . ."

Paul chuckled. "Get ready bro." He patted Derrick on the back. "Pretty soon, she'll take you to meet the parents."

Derrick felt his face heat up. "I already know them . . . We've been friends for years."

Paul shrugged, "Fine then. Take her to meet yours."

Derrick growled. His parents were the last thing he wanted to talk about. He just found out that his father was alive and Ernesto tried to keep hiding the truth from his mom.

Paul backed off. "Whoa . . . Okay . . . What's wrong dude?"

Derrick shook his head. "I'll tell you when we get there . . . I'll just feel a lot better when Cass is here . . ."

Lowe frowned, "I am sorry man . . . I bet you had a rough day."

Derrick shook his head. "No . . . Just a rough afternoon." He just fiddled around with his thumbs.

Raul pulled into Cassidy's driveway where she waited. "Well, we are here man. Maybe now you can tell us what's biting you?"

Cassidy opened the door and squeezed in next to Derrick. "Hello!"

Derrick gave her a hug. "I HAD THE WORST AFTERNOON EVER!" He cried.

Paul just watched with wide eyes, "Okay . . . So it's worse than we thought, huh?"

Cassidy hugged Derrick. "Hey . . . What's wrong Derrick?"

Derrick sniffled and looked up. "He . . . He's alive . . ."

Cassidy cocked her head. "Who?" Her eyes widened. "Your dad?!"

Derrick nodded. "Ernesto's been lying to my mom and me for seven years . . . A-And my mom doesn't believe me, and I am not allowed inside the hospital to see her, and . . ."

Raul pulled out of the driveway. "Okay, Derrick. I think you should start from the beginning man . . . We have a twenty-five-minute drive. Just use the time to vent, okay?"

Derrick sniffled and nodded and started from the beginning and told them about how his dad had gone off to war, all the way to finding the notes and being told to leave the hospital. He told them how angry and hurt he felt and said some things he probably shouldn't have, but they understood.

Paul patted him on the shoulder and Cassidy hugged him. "I am sorry, Derrick . . . I cannot believe that Ernesto would do something like that to you and your mother."

Lowe growled. "That is just messed up. You should find a way to contact your dad. He needs to know this is going on."

Derrick sighed. "I don't know how . . . I don't have the notes, so I can't write . . . and I lost my job, so you can bet Ernesto will let me nowhere near his house . . . so I don't think that I'll be getting the address or the letters . . . All I can really do is hope that he comes home soon." He hung his head. He showed Paul and Cassidy his watch. "He gave this to me for Christmas before he left. I haven't been able to wear it till now because my arms were too small. But I always look at it every single day." He started to cry again. "I thought he was dead . . . I thought he was dead . . ."

Paul comforted him. "It's okay, big guy. It's okay. He will be back one day . . ."

Raul pulled into the parking lot of the Burger Binge, which was alive with activity. He turned off the car and turned to face Derrick. "Man . . . I know that this may not help at all . . . but maybe you should try living life like you dad is coming home soon and you want the first time he has seen you in forever to make him see that you are happy with your life." He smiled and got out of the car. "What better place to start than an all canine party?"

Derrick wiped his eyes. "Okay. Cool . . . Let's go."

Derrick and the others sat at a corner booth sipping sodas or milkshakes. The other booths were overflowing with customers, all of them canines . . . Except Paul and Vinnie, of course. Vinnie had a ball going in between working in the kitchen to coming out and talking hunting and tattoos with some wolves. At one point, Derrick saw Vinnie lift up the back of his shirt to show off a huge wolf head tattoo. The wolves apparently were impressed and offered to help him out with the food in exchange for going on a hunting trip with them.

By the time Derrick and his friends had finished three refills of drinks, Vinnie came over. "Sorry about the wait, lovebirds and friends." He winked at Cassidy and Derrick, who both looked in different direction, a little embarrassed. He took out his pad of paper. "What can I get'cha today? As you can already see, drinks and milkshakes are free, and food is half-off unless you get a special, which is $7.95."

They all ordered their food, and Vinnie wrote it all down, then looked at Derrick. "Okay, Frowny Face. What's up?"

Derrick sighed. "It's a long story . . ."

Vinnie sighed. "I have more experience in long stories than you think. So, when I come back, you can tell me about it." He walked back into the kitchen to give the orders to the new temporary kitchen staff.

Derrick watched as he walked away, then turned to the others, "How is he gonna be able to help?"

Raul smiled. "That cat is actually really good at listening and offering solutions to problems. He'd actually give you pretty good advice about how to fix it."

Paul nodded. "Yes. He used to go to school with us. He's a really good guy."

Lowe nods. "Uh . . . Yeah! Everything he said."

Derrick sighed. "Well . . . if you are sure . . . I'll give him a try." He sighed and sipped his drink.

Cassidy put her arm around him. "It'll be okay Derrick. Maybe he'll give you some ideas to get your mom to see you are telling the truth."

Derrick leaned his head on her shoulder. "I hope so . . . I really would like to get over this so I can be happy my dad didn't actually die . . ."

Cassidy smiled and hugged him. "It's okay, Derrick."

Vinnie came back to the table with their food and sat down next to Derrick. "Okay. So, are you gonna tell me what's up, or are you gonna make me beg?"

Derrick sighed and retold everything that he had told the guys and Cassidy on the way there. As he finished, Vinnie nodded and gave a thoughtful look. Derrick got worried after he didn't say anything for a full minute.

Vinnie sighed. "Wow, man . . . That sounds rough. Your stepdad . . ."

Derrick interrupted. "He has no right to be called that. I think "Jerknesto" is a more accurate name for him now."

Vinnie glared. "Okay then. But next time, don't interrupt." He cleared his throat and continued. "Jerknesto . . . sounds like a tough guy to crack. By the way you talk, I assume you want to expose everything he's done?"

Derrick nodded. "Yes. Especially to my mother."

Vinnie put his paw to his chin. "Hm . . . You could publically humiliate him in some way . . . Scream it in the streets or something . . . I'd do it with some sort of creative flair." As he said the word "flair", he did jazz hands.

Derrick cocked his head. "How would I do that? I have no idea how I would do that . . ."

Cassidy's eyes lit up. "I may have an idea."

Derrick turned to look at Cassidy. "What is it Cassidy?"

Cassidy smiled with an edge. "You aren't gonna like it, Derrick. Last time, you stormed out on me . . ."

Derrick's eyes widened. "The acting competition?! Oh . . . I don't know if I can do that, Cass . . ."

Vinnie stopped him. "She has a point. The theater, Jerknesto's theater . . ."

Derrick cut him off again. "My DAD'S theater."

Vinnie glared. "YOUR dad's theater . . . Whoever it belongs too. It's gonna be filled with people. Jerknesto will be there to see his theater is being put to good use. Perfect opportunity to give evidence with a theater full of witnesses."

Cassidy put a paw on Derrick's shoulder. "If you don't feel comfortable on the stage . . . I understand that."

Derrick winced. "It's not that I don't feel comfortable . . . It's just that I am worried about what other people would think . . . I mean, I haven't really acted in a while . . ."

Cassidy gave him a look. "Oh really, Mr. Phantom?"

Derrick grinned sheepishly. "Okay . . . I mean professionally acted . . ."

Vinnie gave them both a look. "Uh . . . So, I am officially lost."

Derrick sighed. "Looooooooonger story . . ." He chuckled, then turned back to Cassidy. "I think I will go into the acting competition . . . But it's almost here. It's in three weeks. How are we going to prepare in time?! I don't even have any material to go off of..."

Vinnie sighed. "Well obviously if you plan to do that, you are gonna need help, lots of it . . ." He chuckled nervously and gave Derrick a smile. "And a writer?"

Paul kicked Derrick under the table and whispered loudly. "Say yesssssss! He is the best writer in town."

The other five people at the table laughed. Derrick smiled. "Okay then. Looks like I am entering the acting competition."

Cassidy cheered. "Yeah!"

Vinnie smiled. "Sweet!" He wrote down his number on a napkin. "Okay, so Derrick, you need to get as many friends as possible. Also, you need to see if your ex-employer can get those letters back for you. I am already forming the idea for a short skit you can perform using the letters." He slid the napkin to Derrick. "When you have something organized, call me up, and I can probably have something by then. Also, feel free to share this number with any other friends you think could help in my writing of this script."

Derrick nodded and slipped the napkin into his pocket. "Thanks, Vinnie. I'll do just that. Oh!" He took out his phone and showed Vinnie Nathan's number. "This is the number of the guy who can get you those letters."

Vinnie nodded and typed the number into his phone.

He smiled and looked at his watch. "Wow . . . It is late. Frankie and Rowley are probably freaking out, wondering if I died."

Derrick's phone buzzed almost in response to that. Derrick took it out of his pocket and chuckled. "That is not a coincidence." He answered it. "Heeeeello?" He had to pull the phone away from his ear because Rowley yelled so loud.

"WHERE THE HELL ARE YOU, MATE?! Ernesto texted us sayin' you got fired, and we were really, really worried about you, so we have been tryin' to find you. Are you okay?"

Vinnie chuckled. "Man . . . You have some loud friends . . ."

Derrick smiled. "Hey, Rowley . . . I am fine; I am just hanging out at the Burger Binge with some friends from Wolfglade for the dog's night out . . . And yes . . . I found out some stuff about Ernesto that you will not believe . . ."

Rowley kept quiet for a minute. "Ernesto? Wolfglade? Dog's night out? Mate, you have a lot to explain. Frankie and I are coming there now."

Vinnie grabbed the phone. "Dude! What part of DOG'S night out do you not understand?!"

Paul gave him a look. "You aren't a wolf, Vinnie. I keep trying to tell you that."

Vinnie glared at Paul. "No. You aren't a wolf. I was born and raised wolf. I am a wolf at heart."

"Who is that?" Rowley's voice came from the phone.

Vinnie answered. "Oh! It's Vinnie! I am the grill-master from Burger Binge! Hello! I am just giving your friend some advice for a situation he is having."

Rowley stayed quiet for a while then Frankie's voice answered, sounding really hurt. "Why did he come to you for advice? Why didn't he tell us something was wrong?"

Derrick hung his head. "I'm sorry, Frankie . . . I didn't mean to not tell you . . . I was really sad at the time . . . Then the Wolfglade guys called and invited me to come here to talk . . . You guys were gonna be the next to know . . . Cassidy is here, too, she can attest that I am not intentionally trying to ignore you . . ."

Cassidy leaned toward the phone. "He's telling the truth, guys . . . He's just had a bad afternoon."

Frankie sighed. "Well . . . can I still come? I want to be there for you man . . . I promise I won't make any hurtful comments about canines . . ."

Elena's voice came on the line. "I'll smack him before he does."

Derrick looked over at Vinnie with big, sad eyes. "Pleeeeeeeeeeeeease?"

Vinnie groaned. "No way! My customers aren't gonna be happy . . . and my main priority is that they stay happy."

Derrick gave him a look. "I will pay full price for whatever they order."

Vinnie nodded. "As I was saying, I'll go make sure no one tries to throw them out."

The rest of the day went well. Rowley, Frankie, and Elena came by and listened to Derrick's problem and Vinnie's advice. They completely agreed with it and apologized for getting mad at Derrick and introduced themselves to the Wolfgladers. Then, they went home after Derrick said several more times that he would use Vinnie's advice.

Chapter 13

"**S**O, HOW DOES THAT SOUND?" Derrick shared his plan that had been inspired by Vinnie's advice with his table, which now included Vinnie. "We'd all have a part in it. And some of us would even have a shot at an amazing opportunity."

Vinnie smiled. "I am really impressed by this idea, Derrick. Good way to apply my advice."

Conner just looked confused. "Is anyone else still wondering who the heck this guy is?" He pointed at Vinnie.

Vinnie glared at him and made his voice deep and scratchy. "I'm Batman."

Frankie shook his head. "No . . . Cain is Batman . . ."

Cain gave him a side glare. "Are you really gonna make a conspiracy theory out of this?"

Frankie nodded. "Yep."

Buck cocked his head. "Does this mean we can help?"

Manny nodded. "Oh, does it? I wanna help! Please?"

Derrick smiled. "Sure! You guys can be in the skit if you want to be."

Vinnie nodded. "I do need seven characters. You two would be good for two of them."

"YES!" They high pawed each other. "We're totally in."

Derrick grinned. "Awesome!" He cocked his head at Cassidy, who glanced at him with a smile. He smirked a little. "What are you looking at?"

She smiled. "I can't believe you actually agreed to be in the acting competition."

Derrick smiled. "Well, I had motivation this time . . ." He giggled.

She smiled and hugged him. "I'm glad. You deserve this opportunity . . ."

Derrick smiled. "I am glad one of us thinks so."

She chuckled and softly whacked the back of his head. "You are a natural at this kinda thing. You'll do great!"

Derrick hugged her again. "Thanks, Cass." He looked around at the table, watching everyone talk and eat. Conner watched Alex and Vinnie as they wrote the script for the skit. Buck and Manny sat, chatting happily with Rowley and Elena, and Frankie wrote a list of reasons why Cain was Batman while Cain watched with an amused expression.

Suddenly, Derrick felt an urge to go to the bathroom. He turned to Cassidy. "I'll be right back . . ." He got up and walked out of the cafeteria. He walked through the hallways towards the nearest bathroom, the one that was conjoined with the football team's locker room.

As he walked, he smiled. He hadn't felt like this in a while . . . He was genuinely happy. His dad was alive and well. He had a bigger number of friends he would have thought he'd have at this school.

He walked into the bathroom and was about to go into one of the stalls when he heard something come from the direction of the showers. He thought he heard someone crying. He walked into the room where the showers were. "Hello? Is there someone in here?"

As he walked further into the room, he heard a click and turned . . . to see Razor pointing a gun in his face. "Don't move, Hilman."

Derrick gasped. Razor stood beside him holding the gun. But he looked terrible. It had only been a little more than a day since he last saw him, but today, he looked like he hadn't slept in days. His fur was all messed up, and if Derrick wasn't mistaken, Razor still wore the same clothes as yesterday, and he had been crying. "Razor? What happened? Why do you have a gun?"

"Shut up!" Razor prodded him with the gun. "This is all your fault, Hilman! My only friends ditched me to join you! I got detention! My parents argued all night last night, and I couldn't sleep because I frickin' cried all night because I have literally no one left that gives a darn about me."

Derrick put his paws in front of him, showing Razor he wasn't going to do anything. "What do I have to do with any of that?!"

Razor growled, "Because I hate you. I HATE YOU. You came waltzing into our school, got yourself a group of friends so easily, while I only have two! Granted . . . Buck and Manny were . . . are my best friends. And now . . ." He waved the gun around a little. "You've managed to get almost the whole school to hate me, the girl I have been crushing on for a long time to fall for you, and my best friends to ditch me."

Derrick tried to calm him down. "Razor . . . I never meant to do any of that. I never even wanted to go to this school. I had no idea how you felt . . . If you would have just told me, I could have helped you. Buck and Manny still care about you. They are worried about you."

Razor lowered the gun and turned around. "Maybe it's not your fault, then . . ." He sniffled and put the gun to his own head. "Maybe I am aiming at the wrong person." Razor turned to look at Derrick. "This is all my fault . . . I am such a terrible person. I made fun of you every time I saw you, I beat you up, I tried to keep you away from her, and I yelled at my friends when they warned me I was about to go too far, all because I am jealous of you . . ." He put his finger on the trigger. "I don't deserve to live anymore."

Derrick walked forward a little. "Razor . . . Please put the gun down." He put a paw on Razor's arm. "Please . . . Don't do this to yourself. You aren't the one who decides whether you deserve to live or die. That's too big a burden for anyone. But if you want someone to care about you . . . I do. And I am asking you to put the gun down, please . . ." He put a paw on the gun and slowly took it from Razor.

Razor didn't resist and let him take the gun. He just stood there with a sad look on his face. Derrick walked over to the trashcan and threw the gun in it. He looked back at Razor. "Are you okay now?"

Razor nodded and walked forward and hugged Derrick. "Th-Thank you, Derrick . . . I am s-so sorry about how I treated you . . . Please be my friend . . ."

Derrick smiled and hugged back. "Of course, I will, and I forgive you."

Razor broke away after a few minutes and put on a more serious face. "Dang . . . I kind of smell bad . . . I think I am gonna go take a shower."

Derrick chuckled. "Well, you know where to find me." He smiled and walked to the door leading out of the bathroom. Then he realized he didn't do what he came there to do. Oddly enough, however, he didn't really have to go anymore. He shrugged and walked out.

Derrick got back to the table and everyone laughing at a piece of paper that Frankie desperately had been trying to get back. "What is going on here?"

Frankie gave him a pleading look. "Please tell them to give me my paper back!"

Derrick sighed. "Okay . . . What is on the paper, Frankie?"

Frankie flinched a little. "Reasons I think Cain is Batman . . ."

Derrick sighed. "You know Batman is one . . . a comic character, and two, a human, right, Frankie?"

Frankie nodded. "Yeeeeeeah . . ."

Derrick sighed. "Okay, and do humans exist?"

Frankie sighed. "No . . ."

Derrick grabbed the piece of paper from Elena and held it in front of Frankie. "So, what does that mean?"

Frankie frowned. "That Batman isn't real . . ."

Derrick shook his head. "Nope. It just means he's hiding. Come on man."

He smiled and handed the paper back to Frankie, who grinned and went back to his seat. Derrick went to sit next to Cassidy. "Sooooo, we may have an unexpected guest sitting at our table."

Rowley looked up. "Oh yeah? Who?"

Derrick hesitated and decided to ignore Rowley's second question. "Yeah . . . I have to ask you guys to be nice to him . . . He's had a rough two days . . . Try and be friendly . . ." He glared at Elena and Cain. "That goes for you two, especially."

Cain narrowed his eyes but didn't say anything.

Alex went ahead and repeated Rowley's second question. "Who is it?"

Derrick ignored the question and smiled when he saw Razor walk into the cafeteria looking slightly skittish. "Oh, look, here he comes now!" He waved at Razor, who nervously waved back.

Buck and Manny shot up from their seats. "RAZOR!" They ran to hug their friend, who was very happy to see them.

Derrick could feel almost everyone at the table, maybe even the whole cafeteria, looking at him, but he ignored them.

After at least thirty seconds of silence, Rowley spoke up. "You invited . . . Razor? To eat with us? AND HE SAID YES?!"

Derrick gave him a fake annoyed look. "Yeah, and you are speaking in incomplete sentences. Shame on you."

Frankie looked up from his paper and chuckled.

Elena reached across the table and grabbed Derrick by the collar. "Are you crazy?! He hates you! He's been the biggest bully to you. He has physically harmed you. And here you are, flippantly inviting him over for lunch." She shook him a little.

Derrick squeaked because he found it hard to talk with someone holding his collar. "Physical harm? Like what you are doing to me now?"

Elena let go of his collar. "Sorry . . . Impulse . . . I do that whenever people make stupid decisions." She glared at him.

Cassidy gave them both a look. "Shut up you two." She turned to Derrick, "You talked to him, didn't you?" She smiled.

Derrick smiled nervously. "Actually, yes . . ." He chuckled nervously. "I'll tell you later."

Razor came and sat down in the seat next to Derrick and stared down at his food to avoid the looks the others were giving him. "Um . . . Hi." He finally looked up a little.

Cain nodded at him. "Hi."

Razor flinched a little.

Cassidy smiled at him. "Hey, Razor. Glad you could join us."

Razor's ears perked up a little. "Hello, Cassidy . . ." He shot Derrick a nervous glance.

113

Frankie looked around at the others with a hard look. "Oh, you guys are just being rude. Razor, do you wanna see my list of reasons Cain is Batman?"

Razor's ears perked up. "Batman!?" He shot over to Frankie's side. "Yessssssss. That makes perfect sense!"

Frankie, elated that someone had as much enthusiasm about Batman as he did, started taking him through the entire list. Razor listened with enthusiasm that surprised everyone.

The others turned to Buck and Manny for an explanation. Manny smiled, "Oh! Razor is a huge comic book fan. He goes to conventions every single year"

Their eyes got huge as they looked back at Razor and Frankie. "So, wait . . ." Elena started.

Rowley shifted uncomfortably. "Razor's a . . ."

Conner looked shocked. "NERD?!"

Razor's head shot up. "SHHHH! Not out loud . . ." He looked slightly embarrassed. "I don't really like making that known . . ."

Derrick smiled a little. "It's okay. Everyone has a secret hobby . . . Or a not-so-secret secret hobby." He smirked at the others at the table. "Frankie has an addiction to pop tarts, Elena has a secret hobby of going to MMA fights just to yell at the fighters, and Rowley watches chick flicks almost every night before bed."

The others giggled and kept going on talking about silly things like silly addictions and funny quirks. Derrick just let himself forget about everything: Ernesto, his dad, his mom not listening. He felt for the first time in forever like everything would be alright.

Chapter 14

"OKAY." VINNIE SAID, SITTING on the couch in Frankie's living room as he looked at everyone else who had gathered there. "So, I finished the scripts, thanks to some help from Alex and Nathan." He nodded toward them and handed around a copy of the script for them to look at.

Derrick read through the script. "Wow. This is a well-written script. And you wrote this whole thing last night?" He looked closer at the script. "What does the 'Ins. Letters' thing by my lines mean?"

Vinnie smiled. "Well, the letters were really well written, so I thought instead of rewriting them, your characters could act out the letters while we played a pre-recorded track of you reading that letter."

Derrick grinned. "That's a great idea! And Ernesto's name is basically plastered all over it. All we need now is for my mom to be there, and I think I could make that happen. Wait . . . What about props?"

Cassidy nudged him. "Actress remember? I can get you access to the props you need."

Derrick beamed and hugged her. "Thank yoooou! Anyone ever tell you that you are amazing?"

Cassidy smiled. "You haven't let me go a day without hearing it since we met. Except for the last five or six years . . ." She chuckled.

Frankie just shook his head and texted away on his phone, just briefly glancing at the script.

Cain cleared his throat. "So, how many parts are there?"

Vinnie looked at his copy of his script. "Well looking at the letters, there were at least seven other soldiers that he mentions by name. So I need, besides

Derrick, six other guys and a girl." He looked over at Elena and Cassidy.

Cassidy put her paws up, "Don't look at me! I am one of the emcees for the event. I am not allowed to actually act in the plays." She put on a fake pouty face, which got her a hug from Derrick.

Elena chuckled. "Guess that leaves me to take the role." She looked at Vinnie. "Can I punch anyone?"

Vinnie gave her a look. "No. The skits aren't supposed to be violent."

Elena crossed her arms. "When is war not violent?"

"She has a point, mate," Rowley piped up.

Elena patted Rowley's head. "Yes. Listen to the adorable Aussie."

Vinnie rolled his eyes. "And I keep asking myself why I haven't tried to find a girlfriend."

Cain coughed again. "I'll be in it." He looked a little conflicted for a second. "I probably should mention something . . ." He turned to Derrick. "I think my dad is in your dad's unit."

Derrick gave him a wide-eyed look. "What?"

Frankie looked up at that part. "Oh . . . I guess that means you're not Batman . . ."

Cain took a folded-up envelope out of his pocket and showed it to Derrick. "This letter is from my dad. He is stationed overseas . . . He sent me a picture of his squad and . . ." He opened the letter and took out a picture and showed it to Derrick.

Derrick stared at the picture. The second person from the right, standing tall and smiling, was Devon Hilman. He had gotten older, some of his fur had turned grey, but it was still his dad. He still remembered. Derrick smiled and hugged Cain. "Can I keep the picture?"

Cain blinked and put a paw on Derrick's back and patted it. "Uh . . . Well, there is something else . . ."

Nathan interrupted. "Oh, Derrick. Can I see the picture?" He had a look on his face that Derrick couldn't read.

Cassidy had her idea face on. "If we have pictures of them, then we can work on costumes and make-up and stuff."

Cain tried to butt back into the conversation. "Uh . . . guys . . ." Nathan gave Cain a look and motioned for him to follow him outside. Cain gave him a look but followed him.

Derrick watched them leave with a confused expression but went back to listening. Vinnie went on talking about the script. He gave Buck and Manny each a script. "You guys have a few lines each, but they are small, and any other lines, you will say in a low voice so you look like you are in a conversation. It's called background acting."

Derrick smiled at the familiar language. "They would need to do some lower stage whisper. They could have a legitimate conversation, but to the audience, it would need to sound like mumbling."

Vinnie nodded, "Yes. They could probably pull it off." He looked around "Anyone else?" Rowley and Derrick raised their paws. Frankie put a paw in the air but didn't look up from his phone. Conner, being a sneaky little wolf, edged closer to Frankie to try and see who Frankie had been texting since they got there.

Razor watched from the corner of the room. "Umm . . . I would like to be a part of it. I just . . . don't really know how to act."

Derrick smiled. "Well . . . You know how you always try to act tough at school? Key word in that sentence being act."

Razor put on an annoyed face that made him look more like the Razor that Derrick was used to. "That's not acting. I am tough."

Vinnie chuckled. "If you say so."

Buck piped up, "But he is tough! He is a beast at anything that takes physical strength. And that makes up for the fact that he cries when small animals die in movies."

"Hey!" Razor retorted, "They are sad and adorable . . . Sadorable! And you do the exact same thing."

Vinnie thought hard. "Hmm . . . You like being tough, Razor? You could play Ernesto."

Razor thought about it and looked a little reluctant.

Vinnie sighed. "All you'd have to do is act like you did towards Derrick and make yourself ever jerkier."

Razor slowly smirked. "And make him out to be the enormous jerk bag he is? I am in."

Manny raised his paw. "Oh! Can I go get a bag of jerky?"

Buck cringed. "Ewww! You know they sometimes use deer meat to make jerky!"

Manny shook his head. "But it tastes . . ." Buck glared at him, and he shrunk back, "Okay . . . No jerky . . ."

Derrick sighed. "Guys, please . . . We have a play to plan. So, we have me, Razor, Buck, Manny, Rowley, Elena, and . . ."

Cain and Nathan walked into the room, and Cain smiled. "Add me to your list."

Derrick smiled. "Awesome! And of course, we have . . ." He looked at Frankie. "Frankie?"

Frankie chuckled at his phone and typed a message back to the person, obviously not hearing a word any of them were saying.

Conner, who was now close enough to Frankie, snatched the phone and looked at it. "Well, hello. Who is Daniella?"

Frankie reached for the phone. "Give that back!" Conner jumped away, and Frankie fell to the floor. "OW! What's your problem? She's my partner for our English project." He picked himself up and snatched the phone back. "And it's not any of your business."

Derrick sighed, knowing something was up, but he would have to talk to Frankie about it later. But right now, they had a skit to plan. "Can we please just start?"

Everyone nodded, and Vinnie started handing out scripts, and Derrick began studying and practicing with the others. Those who were in the play studied their lines, while Vinnie gave the others backstage jobs like keeping Ernesto off the stage and stuff.

So, they spent the next two weeks practicing for the acting competition, and through the excitement, Derrick had almost completely forgot all about the English project. But somehow, Cassidy had been one step ahead of him, and they had the project finished a week early, which coincidentally ended up being the sign-up day for the Acting Competition. So, Cassidy decided to go hand it in while Derrick went to the table to sign up.

Derrick was going to the table to sign up for the competition when he saw Ernesto standing by the table watching all of the students pass by the table. Derrick cringed and sucked in a breath of air and walked straight towards the table.

Ernesto looked up at Derrick as he walked up to the table. "Well well, look who it is . . ."

Derrick ignored him and looked straight at Turner, who was one of the students in charge of the sign-up sheets. "Hey, Turner. I have a group that has an act together for the competition."

Turner handed him a clipboard, but his face looked a little frightened at Ernesto. "Um . . . Sure, Derrick. Here is a sign-up sheet. I am gonna need the names of the members of your group. And I am also supposed to tell everyone that if your group has more than five people and you are one of the winners, not all of your group will get the scholarship. They have a limited number of those."

Derrick nodded and took the clipboard. "Thank you." He looked at the clipboard, only to have it snatched by Ernesto.

Ernesto handed the clipboard back to Turner, "Sorry son, he isn't able to participate. He has to work that day." He gave Derrick a smug look.

Derrick gave him a smirk back and took the clipboard again, "Um, yeah . . . No. I got fired because I was gonna tell people your secret, and if you try and stop me from doing this, I will get on Frankie's radio station and tell the whole county."

Ernesto gave him an angry look. "You wouldn't do that."

Derrick chuckled. "Oh yes, I would. You aren't making me back out on a chance to act on a stage ever again."

Ernesto growled. "You son of a b . . ."

Derrick interrupted and put a paw over Ernesto's mouth, "Excuse me, sir. We do not use that language in a high school. And I am sure you aren't thinking of either of my parents, because if you were to call either of them that, I might get arrested for putting your thick skull through a wall."

Ernesto growled, "Fine. Put on your little play. I don't care." He walked away. "What harm could a play do, except embarrass you, of course?"

Derrick chuckled. "More harm than you think, Ernesto. More harm than you think." He quickly signed the form and gave the clipboard back to Turner, who stared at him. He swatted at his face. "Is there something on my face?"

Turner shook his head. "No . . . But what you just did . . ."

Derrick sighed. "Maybe that came out a little harsh, but I don't regret it. So, love me, hate me, whatever. I am not taking crap from him anymore."

Turner gave him a look. Derrick cocked his head, "What?"

Turner sighed. "You didn't let me finish."

Derrick gave him a sheepish look. "I'm sorry . . . What were you saying?"

Turner cleared his throat. "I was saying . . . What you did was . . . AWESOME! Man, you told him good and then had him crawling away like a scared puppy. Dude, that was fierce!"

Derrick smiled. "Oh . . . Thank you. I was honestly terrified that he was going to keep going. I almost ran out of gutsy things to say." He chuckled. "Very convenient that he stopped when he did."

Turner cocked his head. "Yeeeeeah. It is."

Derrick chuckled. "Eh, probably just a coincidence."

Turner shrugged. "Yeah . . . But I am gonna need you to get out of line now . . . There are people waiting behind you."

Derrick turned and saw several others waiting impatiently behind him. "Oops . . ." He stepped out of line and awkwardly walked off. "Sorry!"

Derrick stood in front of the mirror in the school restroom after school, practicing his lines for the competition and reading off the letters as needed. He had already pretty much memorized all the lines and the letters, but he wanted to just make sure he had it down perfectly. He still found himself impressed with Alex and Vinnie's writing of the script, which made him vividly imagine what the scene would be like. He hoped that the play would be something that, if his dad saw it, he would be proud of him. He sighed. He had thought about mailing his dad . . . but every time he thought about doing it, something would distract him. He just had to wait for his dad to come home.

His phone buzzed in his pocket, and he picked it up. Cassidy called him. He smiled and answered it with a very enthusiastic, "Hello, Cass!"

She giggled on the other end of the line. "Well hello, Mr. Phantom! How are you today?"

He chuckled. "Why, I am quite well!" He grinned. "What might I do for the lovely Miss Wells today?"

He could hear her stifled laughter. "Well, there is a certain box of costumes that is waiting at Frankie's station, and I am a little preoccupied. Would you mind going to get it? Frankie is in the middle of a broadcast."

He smiled. "Yes, ma'am! I just need to find a ride. I'll probably ask Rowley."

"Okay, great. See you later?" She asked. "We are getting together to rehearse tonight, right? The play is next week."

"Yeah. I remember something about trying to pull an all-nighter. Vinnie said he was bringing food."

She laughed. "Oh. That's sure gonna get you boys there now, isn't it?"

Derrick made his voice sound sad. "Is there something wrong with liking food?"

"Nah." She giggled. "Okay. See you tonight then."

Derrick smiled. "Bye!" He hung up and put his script in his book bag. He headed toward the gym because that would be where Rowley would be. He walked through the door to the gym and looked around. There were several football players working out in there, but none of them were Rowley. He walked over to Razor who was taking point for Conner on the bench press. "Hey, Razor? You haven't seen Rowley around, have you?"

Razor helped lift the weight back up and put the weight on the hook so Conner could sit up. "Yeah. He had to leave, though. Apparently, he has plans with Elena."

Derrick chuckled a little. "Last minute plans?"

Razor smirked. "Yep. She came in and was like 'Hey, let's go get ice cream' and he was like 'Uhh sure.'"

Derrick chuckled "Aw well. Guess I need to find someone else then."

Razor cocked his head. "What'cha need? Maybe I can help?"

Derrick thought about it. "Hmm . . . Yeah, you could. You mind taking me to the radio station? Cassidy said the costumes are supposed to arrive there today and that she wanted me to pick them up."

Razor nodded, "Sure man. I'll take you there. Just let me go shower and change first."

Derrick nodded. "Okay. You do that."

Razor nodded and grabbed his bag and headed off for the showers.

"Sorry about the mess. I usually just drive Buck and Manny around in here." Razor turned the key in the ignition of his truck.

Derrick smiled. "It's okay." He looked around and noticed a lot of stuff that he would never have thought he'd see in Razor's truck. His eyes landed on a CD and widened. "Is this . . ." He picked it up. It was a generic boy band that all the girls listened to. He looked up a Razor with a silly grin

Razor glanced over, and his eyes widened, "NO. NO, IT ISN'T . . ." He took it from Derrick.

Derrick chuckled. "You like . . ."

Razor glared him and interrupted. "Shut up! I don't."

Derrick tried to grab it from Razor. "Don't girls usually like them?"

Razor pulled over on the side of the road and growled. "HILMAN. I swear, if I hear one more word . . ."

Derrick shrunk back. "Okay, man. I am sorry . . ."

Razor smirked and got back on the road. "Please don't tell anyone."

Derrick nodded. "Promise . . ." They both sat in an awkward silence for the rest of the ride. As they pulled up to the radio station, Derrick turned to look at Razor. "Seriously, though, why that one?"

Razor gave him a look, "Oh please, Hilman. You're just jealous that they have more fangirls than you do."

Derrick tried to come up with a good comeback and failed. He sighed. "Yeah . . . Yeah I am . . ." He got out of the car. "I'll be right back . . ."

He walked into the station and looked around. Usually, Turner or someone would be out in the lobby, but no one was there. He looked through the window to the studio and saw Frankie at the mic and Turner watching him attentively.

Derrick shrugged. Frankie usually let Turner sit in while he broadcasted. Nothing that he needed to worry about right now.

As he turned around to look for the box, he rammed into someone, and both of them fell onto the floor. Derrick looked at the other person and was surprised to see the cheetah that he had saved from Frankie's ruthless flirting in the beginning of the year . . . only to start talking to him a few weeks later. He smiled. "Oh. Hello. It's you!"

She cracked a grin. "'Ello. It's you!"

Derrick grinned and stood up, offering her his paw. "Daniella, I presume?"

She grabbed his paw, and he helped her up. "That's me. I assume that crazy bloke talks about me a lot?" She said in a heavy British accent.

He sighed. "A lot less than you think. But from the way he acted when his phone was snatched the other night, it's obvious that you two may be more than English project partners."

Daniella looked down at her feet. "Oh . . . Well . . . Maybe . . ."

Derrick put his paws up. "Hey, I won't say anything. It's none of my business." He smiled. "Besides, you probably want to finish that project . . ." He pointed at the book bag that she had on her back.

Daniella looked at her book bag. "Oh, yes. Very much, actually."

Derrick smiled. "I'll let you go, then. I got a box to find anyway." She smiled and walked into the studio, leaving Derrick to look for the box. He saw the box on the other side of the room and picked it up and made sure it was the right package . . . even though it was the only package in the room. Luckily, he found the right one. Derrick chuckled at how convenient everything had become for him as he took the box out to Razor's truck and got in. "Got the box. Lucky for me it was the only box in the room."

Razor chuckled. "Yeah. That does sound lucky."

Derrick smiled. "We should probably get these to Frankie's house so we can use them for rehearsal tonight."

Razor smiled. "Okay . . ." He cocked his head. "But that is in three hours, what are you doing until then?"

Derrick shrugged. "Probably gonna sit around and play video games." He gave Razor a look. "Wanna join me?"

Razor smiled wider. "If you're okay with it, of course, I want to!"

Derrick chuckled. "Betcha I can whip your tail at wrestling."

Razor gave him a look. "In video games, or real life?"

Derrick crossed his arms and smirked. "Both!"

Razor smirked back. "Oh, you are so on."

Chapter 15

"**T**HIS IS ALL VERY nerve-racking . . ." Derrick peeked out from behind the curtain and looked out at the crowd of people. As far as he could tell, all of the seats in the theater were taken. Derrick looked back around the backstage area at his friends and turned to Frankie and Cassidy. "I don't know if I can do this . . ."

It was the big night. Several very long rehearsals had led to this, and the night had finally come, and Derrick could not stop worrying.

Frankie sighed. "It's gonna be alright, Derrick. You'll do great!"

Cassidy smiled and hugged him. "I know you're an amazing actor. You can do it."

Derrick stuttered. "But what if I mess up?! I'll make everyone laugh at me, but even worse, I will prove Ernesto right and no one will focus on the fact that this is all about exposing him . . ."

Cassidy shook her head. "There is no way you are gonna prove Ernesto right. You wanna know why?" She smiled. "Because he is wrong."

Frankie smiled, too. "Yes. Listen to the husky. I have watched you quote Phantom of the Opera all the way to half of the second act, and that is including the gestures and stuff."

Cassidy nodded. "See? You don't have to be worried about that."

Elena watched them from a few feet away, leaning against the wall in her camouflage uniform for her character, and nodded in agreement. "Seriously. Stop worrying."

Derrick took a deep breath, and then another thought caused to worry . . . AGAIN. "But what if Ernesto tries to stop it?"

Frankie groaned, and Cassidy winced. "I told you already before, Derrick. Your friends from Wolfglade, Conner, and Nathan are going to take care of that."

Derrick nodded, then tried to worry about something else. "B-But...Nathan isn't here..."

Elena finally had enough of Derrick's worrying, walked over, and slapped him across the face. "Snap out of it, Derrick!"

Derrick winced and rubbed his cheek. "OW."

Cassidy also winced. "Elena! That was really unnecessary."

Elena ignored her and glared at Derrick. "No more worrying. Stop it." Derrick opened his mouth to say something, but Elena put a paw up. "Uh. Na. No. Shut up. I said no more. Derrick. You are an amazing actor, and there is no going back. You have already memorized the lines and put on your costume. You are going out on that stage, and you are going to act." She poked him in the chest. "If I hear one more worrisome comment come out of your mouth. I. Will. CUT. You." Derrick opened his mouth again as if to speak, but Elena interrupted him again. "You better not say you can't understand me if I talk in incomplete sentences, because then I will DOUBLE cut you."

Rowley, who had just come up to show them his costume, sighed as he watched her yell. "She is so cute when she's threatening people."

Derrick stood frozen, his eyes wide. "Uhhhhhhh..."

Frankie cocked his head at Derrick. "Derrick? You alright?" He waved a paw in front of his face. "Oh great." He turned to Elena. "I think you broke him."

Cassidy chuckled, "Nah. I think he just needs a hug."

She gave Derrick a hug, and he blinked. "I AM NOT WORRYING!" He said, his eyes wide.

Elena chuckled. "Good boy."

"I told you they were a couple, Chet, I told you." Derrick jumped as he heard his mom's voice come from behind him, and he whirled around. June hobbled towards him on crutches and had a brace on one of her feet. She smiled at him. "You little liar. I should ground you."

Derrick's eyes went even wider than they did with Elena's threats. "Mom?! You are walking!"

June chuckled. "Well of course, I am walking. I ain't levitating."

Derrick was almost speechless. "B-But...They...You...I..."

June smiled. "Apparently, seven years in bed helped me heal. When the doctors saw this, they gave me ten minutes of assisted walking...which was kind of difficult...seeing as how the muscles in my legs hadn't really been used in a while. But I am getting stronger, at least that is what Chet says." She glanced at Chet, "I honestly think he is trying to make me feel less old."

Chet groaned. "You aren't that old."

June smirked. "Always so nice." She turned back to Derrick with a softer expression. "But enough about me . . . I am worried about you. A few weeks ago, you burst into the hospital yelling nonsense about Ernesto being a liar. What's wrong?"

Ernesto came backstage, and when he saw June, he rushed to her side. "June, what are you doing backstage? I told you to stay in the seat" He said calmly but with an easily detectable edge.

June gave Ernesto a look. "I am talking to my son. I may have married you, Ernesto, but that doesn't mean you can keep me from talking to my son."

Ernesto sighed and gave Derrick a nervous look. "But . . . The competition is about to start, and you need to get to your seat."

June took out the program. "But the program says Derrick's group is on last. That is plenty of time to talk to him, just for a while."

Ernesto sighed. "But honey, the audience isn't allowed backstage during the competition."

June looked a little annoyed. "Well then, at least give me five minutes. Sheesh, you are such a control freak sometimes." She giggled a little. She turned back to Derrick. "Are you gonna give me a hug or what?"

Derrick smiled a little and wrapped his arms around his mom. "I missed you so much." He looked back at the curtain. He could hear the crowd mumbling and waiting for the competition to start. "I am so nervous." He whispered.

June smiled, "It is okay, Derrick. I'd be scared too if I were in your place." She sighed. "I haven't been on stage in so long, I feel like if I went on right now in front of those people, I would die of fright." She pulled away and smiled at her son. "Break a leg son."

Chet smiled. "And if you actually do break a leg, I am here, so we can get you to the hospital . . . Just in case, you know."

Derrick smiled a little, then chuckled. "I'll keep all that in mind."

June smiled at him then looked at his costume. "What exactly is your skit? A battle?"

Derrick smiled a little. "Actually, it's a tribute to dad and the soldiers who bravely fought with him."

Ernesto's eyes widened while June smiled. "Wow. That is a really nice way to honor your dad's memory." She turned to Ernesto. "Isn't it, hon?"

Ernesto glared at Derrick. "Yes, honey . . ." He turned to her. "Maybe we should just go back to the hospital . . . I don't want you to overstrain yourself."

June nudged him. "What is your problem, Ernesto? Why do you seem so eager to get me away from Derrick?" She gave him a suspicious look. "You are making me think you really are hiding something from me."

Derrick smirked as he watched Ernesto. He would have to make up a big lie to get out of this one.

Ernesto did. His voice softened a little. "I am sorry, June . . . I guess I am just a bit wound up about tonight . . ."

Derrick almost laughed out loud. His mother would surely never believe that. But as he watched his mother's expression soften, he knew that option was unlikely. She put an arm on Ernesto's shoulder. "I am sorry . . . I didn't realize . . ."

Thankfully, Nathan walked into the backstage area and directed Ernesto, June, and Chet out. "The competition is about to start." He gave his dad a smirk. "Only competitors and stage crew are allowed back here, sir."

Ernesto growled but walked out the door. June smiled at Nathan, then gave Derrick another hug. "We'll catch up afterward, then maybe we could go get some ice cream and ditch the workaholic?" She winked.

Derrick chuckled. "That is the best idea ever!" As his mom left the backstage area, Derrick turned to Cassidy and Frankie. "Maybe instead of ditching that joker just for ice cream, she'll ditch him for life. Gosh, I really hope that conveniently happens."

Nathan sighed as he walked up behind Derrick. "You and me both."

Derrick turned to Nathan. "Where've you been?"

Nathan smiled. "I had to pick up some friends from the airport."

Derrick saw that he was clearly hiding something, but he couldn't tell what. So, he decided to just change the subject. "You have the letters for me, right?"

Nathan smiled and took the letters out of his pockets. "Yup. Here they are." He handed them over to Derrick. "Read them in the exact order they are organized in. You know . . . So, you don't mess up."

Derrick took the letters. "Thanks." He put them into his pocket. He went to where Razor, Buck, and Manny were and just started chatting.

Vinnie stomped up to Nathan. "You better have a good reason for being late. You could have cost us the entire skit."

Nathan gave him a look. "I just said that I was picking some friends up from the airport. What part of that is hard to understand?"

Vinnie crossed his arms. "You should have said something, then. Then I wouldn't have been running around for the past ten minutes, worrying that everything we worked on might fail!"

Nathan scratched the back of his head. "Well . . . these people are kind of important."

Vinnie grabbed Nathan by the collar of his shirt and shook him. "WHO COULD BE MORE IMPORTANT THAN MY SKIT?!"

Nathan slowly detached Vinnie from his collar. "Okay. Number one. This is Derrick's play. You may have written it, but Derrick is the actor. You write the magic; he makes it."

Vinnie sighed, "Fine . . . But you didn't answer my question?"

Nathan slightly lifted the curtain and gestured out. "Look at the back of the room."

Vinnie peeked out and looked. His eyes widened, and he turned to look back at Nathan. "You didn't."

Nathan chuckled. "Oh, I most certainly did."

Vinnie smirked. "You gonna say anything?"

Nathan shook his head. "I'm gonna surprise him. Let him find out himself."

Derrick stood backstage, just sitting on a stool staring at the stage. He had calmed down by now and felt slightly more confident than he had been before. He watched as the lights dimmed and people quieted down.

Cassidy came over to him and hugged him. "Time to go. You can do this."

Derrick smiled and hugged her back. "Have fun."

Cassidy grinned. "Okay . . . Here goes." She walked out onto stage, and the crowd erupted into cheers. "Hey everyone!" She chuckled as everyone yelled and got their excitement out. "How's everyone doing?" The crowd was still flipping out. After a few more seconds of that, she raised her paw to silence the crowd. "Okay. Okay. Let's all quiet down a little, this isn't a rock concert." She smiled as the audience chuckled at that comment. "Okay. So, on behalf of the two schools involved, welcome to the first, but hopefully not the last, Tigerthorn/Wolfglade Acting Competition. Now, as most of you probably know, the top three acts get scholarships to Clayson University of the Fine Arts, which is a huge opportunity, especially for aspiring actors." Again, people cheered. "So, before we get started, I want to introduce our other coordinator for tonight's competition." She smiled at them and gestured to Frankie on the side of the stage he was standing on. "His name is Frankie Christopher, but most of you probably know him better as K-Dawg." That got a whole bunch cheers and clapping.

Frankie walked out onto the stage and took the mic from Cassidy and timidly waved. "Hey guys . . . I know you guys are expecting me to introduce these talented acts tonight, but I am sorry to tell you I am unable to help tonight." Cassidy's eyes widened as she realized she had made a mistake, and she facepawed, and the audience sighed in sadness. Frankie frowned at his audience. "Sorry guys. I am actually a part of one of the acts tonight, though, so you will get to enjoy watching me perform still. So instead of being the coordinator tonight, I am going to introduce you to the one who is. This pup is the one who really deserves the title of DJ K-Dawg. Ladies and gentlemen, please give a warm welcome to the one who helps me keep my studio in perfect shape and my very best sidekick, Turner Phelps!"

Derrick's ears went up as he watched Turner walk onto the stage and take the mic. He had always assumed that Frankie would pass the role onto Turner, but not like this. He watched as the audience stood and clapped as Turner waved. Frankie walked off stage and went to sit next to Derrick with a smile on his face. "The kid is a natural up there, isn't he?"

Derrick nodded, very impressed at the younger pup's ability to talk to a crowd.

Frankie nudged him and chuckled "Hey, one less performance to worry about tonight. Good thing we're up last."

Derrick shuddered. "All I see is more time to worry about what I am about to do."

Frankie chuckled. "Don't worry too much, or Elena will hit you."

Derrick giggled nervously.

The evening went by rather fast, even though Derrick had been worrying constantly about what may, but probably wouldn't, go wrong. Luckily, the act before he had to go on was re-enacting a scene from Shakespeare's "Much Ado About Nothing", and Derrick had watched them with obvious admiration. "Dang! Those two sure know how to Shakespeare!"

Frankie frowned. "You aren't putting yourself down inside your head, are you?"

Derrick turned to give him a look. "No! I know superior acting. And that . . ." He pointed to the two on stage. "Is amazing acting."

Frankie cocked his head, "Eh. I guess."

Derrick shrugged. "I honestly hope that they win."

Frankie smiled. "Well, that's awfully selfless of you."

Derrick smiled. "What can I say? I just like Shakespeare, and these guys just pulled it off quite well." He stood up and clapped as the two on stage bowed and walked off-stage.

Frankie stood up. "You ready? We're up next."

Derrick smiled. "Oh heck, yes." He looked at the other five. "You guys ready?"

Rowley smiled. "Yep," and everyone else nodded along with him.

Derrick sighed. "Okay. Let's do this then."

Cassidy and Turner walked onto the stage as the two went to the backstage area. She smiled. "How about one more round of applause for Dinah and Lance?"

Turner nodded and clapped. "I gotta say, I know I am supposed to be impartial, but WOOOO, that was awesome."

The audience laughed and clapped along, and the judges chuckled at their table.

"I think that the audience agrees, Turner." Cassidy smiled. "But I dunno,

I am kind of more partial to this last one."

Turner laughed. "Because of your boyfriend." The audience laughed and went "Ooooooooh."

Cassidy gave Turner a playful nudge. "Anyway, for our next act, we have Derrick Hilman, Frankie Christopher, Elena Salazar, Rowley Manchester, Razor Channing, Buck Wilder, Manny Kershov, and Cain Michael!" She clapped as Derrick and the others walked onto the stage. "Hello, Derrick, and very big crew."

Derrick smiled. "H-Hey, Cass." He waved at the audience. "Hey guys!"

Cassidy smiled and handed him the mic. "So, I know you have something great planned for tonight, so take it away." She walked off the stage, followed by Turner.

Derrick turned to the crowd, and the others lined up on both sides of him, three on each side and Cain in the back. Derrick took a deep breath as all the lights went off and a huge spotlight hit him. He knew that the others, meaning Conner and Vinnie, were setting up the scene in the dark behind him, so he looked up at the crowd with a serious face. "The events that this skit is based off of were real and serious events. These events were derived from letters from Devon Hilman, my father, who was a soldier."

Derrick passed the mic to Razor, who stood directly next to him. Razor took the mic, "Seven years ago, Ernesto Claw came home to the city of Tiger-thorn, claiming to have been the only survivor of a terrible massacre, but as we have found out and will soon show you, he lied."

Razor passed the mic to Buck. "The letters from Derrick's father were sent to Derrick, but sadly, he never got them. It was all a cover up to hide what Ernesto truly is."

Buck handed the mic to Manny, who stood at the end of the row. "A traitor and a coward. He betrayed his country, his brothers and sisters in arms, and his friends."

Manny passed the mic back down the line to Frankie, who stood on the other side of Derrick. "This skit will cover the seven years Devon and his fellow soldiers went through with no contact from their families and everyone thinking they were dead."

Frankie passed the mic to Elena. "We do this to pay tribute to their sacrifice for our country and to expose Ernesto's cowardice for abandoning his fellow soldiers."

Elena passed the mic to Rowley. "So, in honor of these soldiers, we ask that no one get up, seeing how you will draw a lot of attention to yourself and away from the story."

Cain took the microphone from Rowley and gave the audience his signature glare. "You respected the other acts, now please give us the same privilege and enjoy our skit."

The stage went completely dark. Then the stage lights came on, and everyone sat in a circle with tents and barrels around them. Derrick smiled at the letter and began pretending that he was scribbling on the paper, and he began reading. "Lieutenant Devon Hilman, to my son Derrick Hilman. Dear Derrick..."

Ernesto stood near the side of the theater nervously. The little brats were telling the people everything. He looked at June and saw that she looked really ticked off. He had to stop this and turn it around on those delinquents. He walked up to the door to the backstage area while avoiding dirty looks from several members of the audience. He opened the door, only to find Raul, Paul, and Lowe in their Wolfglade leather jackets and Security Caps. For a moment, Ernesto was impressed. "Wolfglade? You guys are security guards?" The three football players nodded. Ernesto shrugged. "Hm. They made the right choice."

Paul smirked. "Yes. We ain't lettin' anybody in here."

Ernesto nodded. "Good show, Wolfglade." He tried to walk through the door, but got pushed back by all three of them. "What?" He gave them a look. "Come on, not funny. Let me in."

Raul smirked. "Sorry sir. We have our orders from Mr. Claw that no one can come backstage unless they are a part of the acts."

Ernesto gave them a look. "I'm Mr. Claw. I gave no such orders."

Lowe chuckled. "You may be the Mr. Claw who owns the theater, but we have our orders from the manager. And he specifically said to not let anyone in."

Ernesto muttered and took out his wallet and pulled out three fifty-dollar bills, then put his wallet back in his pocket. "Okay kids, how much you want. I'll give you fifty bucks to let me in."

Paul's eyebrows raised, and he took a step closer. "Each?"

Ernesto smirked. "Each."

Paul laughed and shook his head, stepping back. "Nope. Bribery will not work on me."

Ernesto growled, turned around, and walked away.

Paul chuckled and closed the door. "That was fun."

Lowe gave him a look. "Oh yeah?"

Paul pulled Ernesto's wallet out of his back pocket. "Oh yes, it was." He leafed through it. "He got so absorbed in trying to bribe us that he is walking around with three fifties but no wallet to put 'em in." He chuckled.

The other two rolled their eyes but snickered along with him.

Meanwhile, Ernesto walked around to the other side of the theater, trying to find a way to get back stage. He went to the exit on the right side of the theater and reached for the door, only to have his paw grabbed by scaly claws. He turned to see Gus standing next to him. "Where'd'ya think you're going?"

He gave Gus a distasteful look. "Who the hell are you?"

Gus tightened his grip on Ernesto's arm. "Is that anyway to talk to your former superior officer, Claw?"

Ernesto backed away when he recognized the old lizard. "Captain Silviano?"

Gus grinned with a smirk. "That's more like it, deserter."

Ernesto backed up even further. "Who let you in?" He kept backing up until he backed into someone.

"I did." The person behind him growled.

Ernesto whirled around, and his eyes widen. "No . . . NO! Anyone but you!"

Derrick was surprised at how well the play had been going. He could tell by the audience's reaction that they were buying the performance. Ernesto would not ever have a good reputation ever again. They were just about to finish the last page of the script Vinnie had written, when he noticed that he still had one letter left to read. He was a little confused because he had just read the last letter of the skit. As the scene ended, and everyone got ready to get up and take a final bow, he began to read.

"Devon Hilman, to my son, Derrick Hilman." Derrick's voice stopped as he saw that the letter had today's date. He swallowed and tried to start reading again. He could hear the others behind him whispering to each other, probably wondering what the heck was going on. "Dear Derrick, it's good to know that you finally got my letters, kiddo. I have heard you've been doing a lot of stuff since I have been gone. I also have heard that, apparently, everyone thinks I am dead. Well . . . obviously, since you are probably reading this letter on a stage in a theater full of people, you probably know that I am not." Derrick chuckled a little but still couldn't wrap his mind around how he could've known what was going on in his life. He continued reading. "It sometimes got really lonely when we were over there . . . So, any chance of laughter or fun needs to be remembered, and a chance to come home should never be turned down . . . You know what? To hell with this vagueness. Kid, I am coming home. I am coming home to you, your mother, and I am going to make up for all those years that I haven't been there for you, kid." Derrick sniffled and was about to cry. He could hear complete silence coming from behind him as he kept reading. "And I am as sure as hell gonna have scared the heck outta Ernesto at least once by the time you've read this letter. So, to finish this last letter to you off. I love you son. I love you and your mom so very much. Signed, Devon Hilman" Derrick couldn't hold it anymore, and he cried on stage. As he wiped his eyes, he saw that there was a P.S on the letter. As he read it, his eyes widened. "P.S. When you get done crying I am gonna need you to look up, kiddo."

Derrick's eyes shot up, and he scanned the crowd, when he saw eight figures in the back standing against the wall. One of them, a timber wolf with slightly grayed hair, raised his paw to his forehead and saluted. Derrick dropped the letter. "D-Dad?" The timber wolf in the back beamed at Derrick. Derrick's eyes went even wider, and he jumped off the stage and ran to his dad. "DAD!"

Devon smiled and opened his arms. "Hey kiddo!"

Derrick ran into his dad's arms and hugged him. "Oh my gosh! You're here. You're really back!" He pulled back. "I missed you so much." Derrick suddenly got the feeling he was being watched, and then he realized he had just interrupted an acting competition, but you know what? He didn't care. His dad was home.

Suddenly, Cain rushed over, hugging the rabbit next to Devon. "DAD!"

The rabbit chuckled and hugged back. "Hey, Cain." He gave his son the once over. "Dang, you've gotten big. How much you bench?"

Derrick watched this exchange with wide eyes. Devon chuckled, "Surprised? Cain is adopted. Kenny was always telling us about his little pup Cain."

Derrick cocked his head. "Cain used to be short? Add that to the list of things that I have learned this year."

Cassidy and Turner walked back on the stage, "Umm, okay . . ." Turner said. "While that touching moment happens, we are gonna take a ten-minute break so the judges can come up with the winning acts."

The crowd started moving around, talking to each other and doing stuff.

Cassidy walked off the stage and headed toward the small group that had formed in the back.

When June saw her son jump off the stage and run back, she knew right then what it meant. She turned, and there he was. It was true . . . Devon was alive. Which meant that Ernesto had lied to her. She turned to Chet. "Chet. Give me my crutches."

Chet looked at her. "June, we still don't know if your legs are strong enough to walk that much."

June gave Chet her the glare every mother gives an annoying or disobedient child. "Chet. That is my husband back there. You better help me get there, or so help me I will . . ."

"Got it." Chet nervously handed her the crutches and helped her up out of her seat. "Okay, Mrs. June, slowly now."

June didn't pay any attention to his caution. She walked with the crutches down the aisle to Devon. "Devon!"

Devon turned away from Derrick and looked at June. "June!" He ran to her and gave her a nice, gentle hug. "I got a letter explaining everything. I am so sorry about the accident. I should never have left you."

June cried. "I should never have believed Ernesto." She hugged him super tight.

Devon also cried. "I am not mad at you for marrying him. You had no idea." He turned to Ernesto, who was cowering between two of the other soldier. "I AM extremely mad at you." He got in Ernesto's face. "You took my wife, you turned my kid into an underpaid employee, and you deserted us in the middle of a war!" He growled. "You know what I should do to you right now, buster?"

Ernesto pressed himself against the wall. "I-I don't know . . . but I really don't want to find out . . ."

Devon stepped closer. "Good call, because you know what? I ain't gonna do it. Because I can forgive you." He stepped back a little, and June hobbled forward and slapped Ernesto. "Of course, I can't control what she does."

Ernesto hid his face. "I am sorry . . . I am so, so very sorry. I deserved it."

Derrick actually began to feel sorry for Ernesto. "Dad . . . What are you going to do?"

Devon sighed. "I don't know, Derrick . . ."

Derrick gave his parents a look. "I think he's been through enough today . . . The slap was unnecessary."

Devon gave June a look. "He's right, hun."

June sighed. "I am sorry about that . . . I was a little angry."

Ernesto squeaked, "A little? That was hard!"

Derrick nodded. "Yeah . . . The purpose of tonight was to just humiliate him. I didn't want him to get hurt. Maybe . . . you could put him to work or something. He doesn't need to get hurt."

Devon crossed his arms and looked at Ernesto. "Can you believe this? He's sticking up for you, so I'd take this opportunity. I'll let you work as an employee here at the theater, and you can take over as janitor."

Ernesto gave Derrick a grateful look. "Yes. I take it. Thank you, Derrick. Thank you very much."

Derrick nodded. "You're welcome. This doesn't change the fact that I am still mad at you for the past seven years."

Ernesto chuckled nervously. "Noted . . . Duly noted." He turned to Devon. "My daughter helped make Derrick's life miserable, as did Razor."

Devon growled. "Blame-shifting?

Derrick sighed. "Razor and I are okay, though. But Lorena was a pretentious jerk in almost every single way."

Devon gave Ernesto a look. "Okay. Fine . . . You both can start after this event is up." He turned to Nathan who had just walked up. "Your son, on the other hand, informed me that you've had him heading up managing affairs here?"

Ernesto nodded. "Yes. He is very skilled at it."

Nathan shyly smiled. "I just like crunching numbers and organizing stuff, I guess . . ."

Devon smiled. "Tell you what, if you contact me sometime in the next three days, you can keep that position permanently."

Nathan beamed. "Really?" He shook Devon's paw. "Thank you, sir. Thank you very much."

Derrick ushered forward his friends. "Dad, these are my friends." He pointed at each one of them. "This is Frankie, Rowley, Elena, Conner, Alex, Vinnie, Razor, Buck, Manny, Raul, Lowe, Paul, Turner, and of course, you apparently already know Cain." He saw Gus standing off to the side and gave Gus a hug. "Hey, Gus!"

Gus smiled and gave Derrick a hug back. "Hey kid."

Derrick heard someone clear their throat and turned. "Oh!" He went and put his arm around Cassidy. "And this is Cassidy."

Cassidy smiled. "Yeah, you better not forget about me, Mr. Phantom."

Devon smirked as he gave Cassidy the once-over. "Oh my! What a beautiful girl." He put paw to his chin. "Hmm . . . She's a husky, though." He looked at Derrick, "I thought I raised you wolf."

Derrick and Cassidy looked at the ground and fidgeted a little. June gave him a look. "Devon. You have literally been back for five minutes, and already you're goofing off?"

Devon gave her a sneaky smile. "Still . . . She is something."

Derrick groaned. "Daaaaaaad!"

Cassidy chuckled. "Nice to meet you, too, Mr. Hilman." She looked over at the stage and saw that the judges were standing on the stage. "Oh, Turner. We have to go announce the winners." She gave Derrick a kiss on the cheek. "Good luck!" She and Tanner ran to the stage.

Derrick turned to his dad. "We'll catch up after. Maybe we could maybe have ice cream to celebrate?"

Devon smiled. "Sure." He winked. "But don't tell your mother. You know how much she hates it when you are on sugar."

June chuckled, and Derrick hugged his dad. "I missed you so much, Dad."

Devon smiled softly. "I did, too, son. I did, too."

Derrick smiled and turned to follow everyone back to the stage. He just hoped that he had done well enough to impress the judges . . .

Chapter 16

CASSIDY STOOD ON THE STAGE, smiling at the crowd. "Hey guys. I am gonna need all of you to go back to your seats so we can announce the winners of this year's acting competition." She smiled at everyone as they situated themselves.

Tanner smiled. "So, we have had some amazing acts tonight, and the judges loved all of them. But of course, they could only pick three of them to win and receive the scholarships. So, if and when your crew is called, please come on stage to shake paws with the judges and give one last bow." He turned to Cassidy. "You get to do the honors." He handed her the envelope with the winners' names.

Cassidy smiled and opened the envelope and grinned. "In third place, we have Sharon, Keira, and Randy with their re-enactment of a scene from Antigone." The audience clapped as Keira, a German Sheppard; Sharon, a mongoose; and Randy, a fox ran onto the stage and enthusiastically shook the judges and Turner and Cassidy's paws.

Turner smiled. "Congratulations, you guys."

Cassidy smiled. "In second place, we have . . ." She smiled brightly. "Derrick, Frankie, Rowley, Elena, Razor, Buck, Manny, and Cain with a dramatic interpretation of what the judges called 'My Father's Letters.'"

Derrick and the rest of his crew ran on stage. Cassidy smiled and hugged them all, but was taken off guard when Derrick pulled close and kissed her, but of course . . . she didn't complain. The crowd and the people backstage clapped and cheered even louder at that part.

Derrick pulled away. "Sorry . . . Forgot you were working."

Cassidy chuckled. "Yeah. You should wait till later." That made the crowd titter.

Derrick awkwardly went to stand by the rest of his crew.

Turner chuckled. "None of that for me, please."

Cassidy nudged him. "So anyway, we are down to our first-place winners. Aaaaaaand our first-place winners are . . ." She smiled and winked at the crowd. "Dinah and Lance and their re-enactment of a scene from 'Much Ado About Nothing'!"

Dinah, a Siberian wolf, and Lance, a salamander, screamed happily and ran onstage. They shook paws with the judges and Cassidy and Turner, then went to hug the other contestants. Then, as if they all were thinking the same though, all of the contestants came on stage, formed two long lines, and bowed to the audience.

Cassidy smiled and waved to the audience. "Thank you, guys, so much for coming out tonight, and we will see you next year!" The audience clapped respectfully and started heading out of the theater.

Derrick smiled as he chatted with his friends and the other competitors when one of the judges, a white fox, approached him. "Hello. Mr. Hilman, if I am correct?" He smiled. "My name is Andrew Hollister. I am one of the professors at Clayson."

Derrick smiled and shook the fox's paw. "Professor Hollister? I remember you from when I was younger."

The fox smiled. "Yes, as do I, and I must say that your acting skills have excelled far beyond what they were when you were a pup." His smile twitched. "I am afraid, however, we have some bad news."

Derrick and his friends gathered around. "What's wrong, sir?" He asked.

Professor Hollister coughed. "In coming here, we were only ready to offer ten scholarships . . . seeing as how your team has eight people, we can't give every one of you a scholarship."

Razor looked around the group. "Well, I don't need a scholarship, so you don't have to give me one."

Frankie also shook his head. "Already had another college in mind, so count me out."

Cain just grunted. "I am NOT going to acting college."

The professor looked surprised. "Well then . . . That happened. I guess the rest of you are good, then."

Derrick looked around at everyone. "REALLY?! Is no one else seeing how convenient this is?"

The professor handed Rowley, Elena, Buck, Manny, and Derrick each an envelope. "This was purely based on your talent, Mr. Hilman. Convenience had nothing to do with it. We expect to see great things from you and your friends." He shook Derrick's paw and walked back to his fellow judges.

Frankie opened his mouth to say something, but Daniella ran onto the stage suddenly and hugged him. "Oh my gosh, Frankie! You were amazing out there!"

"Thanks, Dani." His ears flattened as the others smirked at him. "This is Daniella. Turns out she is a foreign exchange student from the United Kingdom."

Derrick chuckled. "See! I told you there was a foreign exchange student."

Frankie growled. "Oh, shut up, you didn't know squat, you said the foreign exchange student was a dingo."

Devon and June came on stage, him helping her walk. Devon's face showing mock disapproval. "Second place, Derrick?" He chuckled. "I could've gotten first."

Derrick laughed. "Against someone re-enacting Shakespeare? Good luck with that!"

Devon smiled. "Yeah. Those kids did pretty well. They deserved that first place. But you wanna know something? I woulda picked y'all."

Derrick chuckled. "Oh please, Dad, you would be disqualified for too much bias towards my team."

Devon chuckled. "You bet I would!" He smiled at the crew. "So, we getting ice cream?"

Derrick looked around at all his friends with a playful smirk. "Duh. Of course!"

Derrick smiled as he ate his ice cream. But he wasn't engaging with his friend. He watched his parents, who were standing outside talking, instead. He wondered what exactly they were talking about. Then as he watched, his dad got down on one knee, and his mom smiled as he held on of her paws and spoke to her. He couldn't tell what his parents were saying, but he had a pretty good idea of what they were talking about. After a few minutes, they came in and sat on both sides of Derrick.

Devon smiled. "So . . . Derrick. You know how your mom married Ernesto even though I was still alive?"

Derrick nodded.

June smiled "Well, we talked it over, and seeing as how Ernesto lied to me and since your father is still alive . . . by law, we are technically still married. But luckily, since Ernesto is divorcing me . . ."

Devon smiled and finished for her. "We have decided to get remarried."

Derrick grinned. "Really?!" He hugged them. "That is awesome!"

June smiled. "You bet it is. We are going to plan it for some time around Christmas."

Devon frowned. "Awwwww . . . Does this mean I don't get anything else for Christmas?"

June elbowed him in the side. "Shut up, you!"

Frankie laughed. "Derrick, I had no idea your parents were so funny!"

Derrick chuckled and hugged his parents again. "I had almost forgotten. He used to make jokes like this all the time."

Rowley smiled. "I'll say, mate!"

Devon smiled around the table. "I'd love to get to know all of you better. But of course, any friend of Derrick needs to be screened for murderous tendencies." He chuckled.

Everyone looked at Rowley and Elena. "Uh oh." Frankie said. "Rowley, you and Elena are in troooooouble."

Rowley frowned. "I only threatened him once so he wouldn't wreck Cherry Cola." He growled.

Elena shrugged, "I ain't worried. I could probably take him in a fight." She smirked at Devon.

Devon grinned. "Oh? Could you now?" He put his paws up. "Come at me bro!"

June rolled her eyes. "Devon. No. You are taller and probably weigh two times her weight."

Elena smirked. "But not at video games."

Derrick laughed. "Oh no, the reigning champions are Razor and Cassidy."

Razor smiled. "I get lots of practice at conventions."

Conner cocked his head. "NERDS PLAY VIDEO GAMES?"

Alex and Turner sighed. "Conner, you really need to stop watching movies. They are giving you stereotypes."

Cassidy grinned. "And I am just that good." She smirked.

Derrick smiled as he watched his friends and his parents interact, and for the first time in seven years, he could truly say he was totally and completely one of the happiest animals in the world. Things couldn't be any better.

Chapter 17

So over the next seven months, Derrick graduated high school, and for the summer, he spent as much time with his friends and parents as he possibly could. Then, the next school year came around, and they all had to separate. Derrick, Cassidy, Elena, Rowley, Buck, and Manny went to California to start school at Clayson. But Derrick made sure they all visited home at least once a month to hang out. Frankie and Daniella ended up going to college together in Tennessee, where Frankie got into a music program and started writing his own music. Razor ended up joining Cain in being the coach of Tigerthorn High's football team, and both of them ended up joining the three Wolfglade guys in going to Tigerthorn University. Turner ended up taking over Frankie's job and became DJ Blondfist and took on a roadie of his own, a black cat named Jayson. Conner and Alex just continued life as students, Conner playing football, and Alex writing short stories for the school newspaper.

Of course, they all came back together for Derrick's parents second wedding. And to find that June had healed to the point that she could walk again. But that wasn't the biggest surprise of the night as they soon found out. Derrick had an even bigger surprise for them all.

The wedding reception had been going perfectly. Derrick smiled as all of the guests danced around on the dance floor. He smiled even bigger when Cassidy came up to him and tried to pull him in to dance with her. She was a year older than she was in high school and still the prettiest girl he had ever seen. He smiled and finally agreed to dance with her. He had wanted to do something right now, but he couldn't bring himself to go do it. But for now, he just wanted to dance with Cassidy.

She smiled at him. "You are a good dancer."

Derrick chuckled. "My mother would disagree. She almost gave up teaching me how to dance. I literally couldn't do it until earlier today."

Cassidy chuckled. "It's alright, Derrick. Besides, you are so darn adorable when you are clumsy."

Derrick giggled. "Aww. Gee thanks, Cass."

Cassidy kissed him on the cheek. "No problem, Mr. Phantom." She looked over at his parents laughing at their little table and eating cake. "They both look great and really, really happy."

Derrick smiled. "Yeah." Suddenly, someone bumped into him, and he tripped and fell on the dance floor. He looked up and saw Rowley and Elena.

Rowley looked down at him. "Oh, sorry, Derrick. We didn't see you there!" He helped Derrick up off the floor, then gave him a look. "Hey, did you ever get that present out of your car?"

Derrick sighed. Ah . . . The moment he had been fearing . . . Though . . . it wasn't a bad fear, more like a nervous fear. Rowley was trying to make sure he didn't skip out on the opportunity he had right there and now. "Oh. Thanks for reminding me!" He turned to leave, then looked back at Cassidy. "Cass? Can you come help me with this?"

Cassidy smiled. "Sure, Derrick. Is it big?"

Derrick smiled. "I'd say so." He took her paw, and they walked outside to his car. He smiled as he watched Cassidy walk beside him. She had no idea what he had planned. He smiled as he unlocked the door and opened it.

Cassidy jumped as a bunch of stuff fell out of the car. "Oh my."

Derrick gave a fake groan and knelt down on one knee to pick up the stuff.

Cassidy also knelt down to help. Derrick, instead of picking up the stuff, turned to face her with an open ring box in his paws. "Cassidy Wells."

Cassidy's paws went to her mouth, and she let out a squeal. "Oh my gosh!"

Derrick took her paw. "I have loved you for the longest time. You are literally the only person that has made me lose my words, because you are literally the most beautiful girl I have ever met."

Cassidy looked like she was ready to cry. "That is so sweet . . ."

Derrick smiled. "So I want to know . . . Will you marry me, Cassidy Wells?"

Cassidy nodded. "YES! Oh my gosh, yes!"

Derrick smiled and took the ring out of the box and slipped it onto her finger and stood up.

She grabbed him by the back of the neck and kissed him. Derrick smiled and hugged her.

They were interrupted by the voice of Derrick's dad. "Hey! Whose wedding is this?" Devon smirked and crossed his arms. "The nerve of you two."

Cassidy grinned and pointed at Derrick. "He did it!"

Derrick nodded. "I regret nothing."

Devon smiled and rolled his eyes. "Yeah . . . Excuses." He smiled and came over to them. "I am just kidding." He hugged them both. "My boy has a wedding coming up!"

The wedding guests came outside and surrounded Derrick, cheering and congratulating the newly engaged couple.

Epilogue

As all of the guests gathered around Derrick and Cassidy, Vinnie hung back. He turned away from the crowd and smiled at you, the reader. "So . . . This is how Derrick's year ends. It looks like everything worked out for him, doesn't it?" He chuckled. "Well, Derrick and Cassidy do end up getting married, and they have two beautiful children. Derrick actually ends up calling them wolfskies. Can you believe how silly that sounds? They have a daughter named Jacqueline, and two years later have a son named Jackson. Derrick finally ended up using his talents on the big screen, sometimes alongside his wife. In fact, some of his movies were even nominated for awards, but even with all of that, Derrick was content with his life nonetheless. He had a great family and actually came to love his life again. So that is . . ."

Paul came up next to Vinnie. "Vinnie, what are you doing?"

Vinnie jumped. "PAUL! You interrupted my super cool speech."

Paul sighed. "You know the writer could have done that, right?"

Vinnie sighed. "But I wanted to do this!"

Paul sighed. "NO. Seriously. I know what you are doing. You were going to try to end with a comment of how only a wolf could know all of that. And you aren't a wolf."

Vinnie whined. "Yes, I am!"

Paul dragged Vinnie into the crowd, then peeked out at you, again still the reader, who is probably wondering where this is going. "This is the end of the book. Stop reading now."

About the Author

VINCENZO PASQUARELLA HAS been writing furry-esque fiction for almost a year now, but *The Phantom Janitor* is his first published novel. He hails from the fabulous state of Florida, where he has lived for ten out of the nineteen years of his life. In addition to writing, he enjoys acting, cooking, Hallmark movies, and constantly falling down and pretending he has passed out.(Honestly, he is a little weird like that.) If you would like to find more from Vicenzo and keep up to date on his current projects, you can find him at

https://www.facebook.com/hbcquills/